DISSATISFIED

A novel
By Ksenija Nikolova

KINGSLEY
PUBLISHERS

First published in South Africa by Kingsley Publishers, 2022
Copyright © Ksenija Nikolova, 2022

The right of Ksenija Nikolova to be identified as author of this work has been asserted.

Kingsley Publishers
Pretoria, South Africa
www.kingsleypublishers.com

A catalogue copy of this book will be available from the National Library of South Africa
Paperback ISBN: 978-0-620-98197-2
eBook ISBN: 978-0-620-98198-9

Translator: Nela Trajanoska
Editor: Ferial Mohamed

Dedication

My dear lady, this story is not about the person you are in love with.
This story is not about the people in your life either.
This story is about you, and it's yours only.
In this story - you decide everything.
I hope you decide to be happy.

Yours,
Ksenija

CHAPTER ONE

August 6, 2019

My dear Arthur,

I'm writing this letter to you while you're fast asleep. As I stepped out of the bedroom, I saw you on the sofa downstairs. You looked so peaceful, sleeping in the living room. I envy you for being able to sleep so soundly. You look like a sinless angel, but that's not who you are. The truth is you're an unpredictable devil who feeds off people's souls. You crushed me into a million pieces, now there's nothing left of me. I tried to tell you how much you've hurt me, but my words mean nothing if you don't listen. I may as well be invisible. I certainly know that I'm unimportant. I felt like I was only your shadow, but then I realized that I'm not even that. A shadow is something that is there - you can even fear it, but I'm utterly gone. I don't exist at all.

Let me get back to the reason for this letter. I have decided to leave you, my very charming and handsome husband. I know when you read this you'll think I'm crazy for that - the craziest woman in all of Paris. I'm not the craziest woman in all of Paris at all, I'm only the unhappiest. I'm a woman who has nothing to live for anymore. I wake up and fall asleep with my grief. I lost my identity a long time ago. It's your fault Arthur, you who will so easily replace me when I'm gone.

When you first proposed to me I was so happy. We hadn't known each other for long, but I was sure we belonged together. I was madly in love with you and I couldn't wait to be your wife, but nothing turned out the way I thought it would. After I came to Paris two years ago and we started our life together as husband and wife, it seemed time stopped, turning into an unbearable hell. You work all the time and I'm always home alone. You have a whole life that doesn't include me. What do I have? I have nothing. Silly me, once I even thought you had a mistress, but then it occurred to me that if you don't even have time for your own wife, how would you have time for another woman? If wanting another woman was the problem I would have felt it. Maybe it would have been easier for me then, to know that you were happy with someone else, even if it wasn't me.

Remember, I came to Paris from Roubaix because of you. I left my life there. I left my mother. I left everything because I believed our love could be a beautiful new beginning. But I don't know anyone here. I don't have any friends and I don't have anyone to talk to. My days are completely empty Arthur, but it doesn't seem you even notice. If you do, you don't seem to care. I don't have a job. I don't have any hobbies. I have nothing that fulfills me. That's why I wanted children so badly. When it didn't happen for us, all you said was the universe was telling us it wasn't the right time. Not true, Arthur. You just don't want it as much as I do.

"The most important thing is that neither of us has any medical complications making it impossible to have a baby. We know we're healthy because of the test results, and we should just relax," you said. "You heard the doctors say we haven't been trying that long, one year is nothing. It will happen in its own time. You're only thirty-two years old, and I'm thirty-eight - this isn't our end, it's our beginning, don't force it Margot, let it be. Learn to be happy while you're waiting for what you want," that's what you said every time, and that was the beginning of our end.

We stopped communicating. We stopped touching. We turned into strangers who live under the same roof but live separate lives. We haven't slept in the same bed for months and you seem to have found your peace on the sofa in the living room. I asked you once why you don't sleep on the big bed in the spare bedroom and you smiled and told me that a big bed is too big for one person. That made me sad, but you didn't seem to care. You probably don't even know how much your words hurt me. You just don't understand. It's easy for you because you have a life. It's different for me because I'm so lonely. I can't live like this anymore.

Forgive me Arthur, but it's too hard to go on like this. I need a full life. I'm the kind of person who loves to have new things happening all the time. I want exciting adventures. I want it all. I hate your damn job so much. I know it gives us security, but it also takes you away from me. You think my feelings are silly, right? You don't know what it's like for me. I told you a few weeks ago I wanted to die and you didn't even blink an eye. That's the thing - you don't listen to me Arthur. You don't really listen to me.

While you are sleeping serenely, I can't sleep at all because of the weight of the grief. And when I do fall asleep, I can't wake up because of the heaviness in my heart. That's how it goes, around and around in circles. What's the point of us being together if even one of us is miserable? I don't feel like I'm relevant to you Arthur. Arthur, I hate you.

Yours,

Margot

P.S. Remember how you used to call me Pearl when we first fell in love with each other. You told me that I'm a hidden treasure, just like a pearl. Out of all the things you could have done with that pearl, you chose to destroy it.

CHAPTER TWO

August 7, 2019

My dear Arthur,

Today has been a strange day. This morning while you were getting ready for work, you leaned over me in bed and kissed me on my cheek. I felt you, I wasn't asleep. I opened my eyes to look at you but you didn't say anything. You just smiled at me. When you left, I got up immediately and started packing some of my clothes into a bag. My plan was to go to a hotel and then back to Roubaix. I was worried about my mother who was there alone. Since my father died, she has been so fragile. Sometimes I wish I had a sister or a brother to share my pain with, someone in the same situation as I am, someone who could understand me.

I had packed in a few things when my phone rang.

"What are you doing Margot?" It was my mother, and I worried that something had happened.

"I'm fine Mom, I'm home," I replied. "How are you? Is everything okay?"

"I'm good Margot, everything's fine. What are you up to? Are you busy?"

"I'm at home, Mom. I'm watching something on TV."

"Margot, why don't you go out a bit? It must be so beautiful in Paris and you're stuck in the house. Go out, take a walk. How is Arthur?" Of course she asked about you, as if you are her child, not me.

"He's great, he's working as usual," I said.

"He must be busy. SFR is a huge company, I've seen their new ads on TV and I always think of him when it comes on."

"He's not the only one there, Mom."

"Yes, but Arthur is very hardworking. Tell him I said hello, and tell him to take care," she said.

I didn't want to talk to her anymore so I said we had a bad connection and hung up. You are her darling because she doesn't know how unhappy you make me. She doesn't see how much I suffer because of you. I keep quiet about it Arthur, I keep quiet about everything. Maybe she has a feeling that something is wrong, but she doesn't know the details. She doesn't know about my loneliness. I don't want to worry her because I know what happened with my father nearly destroyed her. She doesn't need to hear about my suffering as well.

I stashed the bag of clothes that I had packed to run away from you at the back of my closet, but then I decided to delay my leaving for another day. I hid the bag behind my summer dresses and as I did so, I noticed my favorite swimsuit hanging on one of the hangers. It made me think back to the time we bought it; it was last year in Antibes. I put it on impulsively, but when I looked at myself in the mirror I felt like I was looking at another person. All I could see was my dull skin, my empty eyes with dark circles under them, and my tired body. I couldn't see the person I once was. I only saw a neglected and unhappy woman. It's your fault, Arthur. I will never forgive you for making me lose myself!

As I'm writing this letter you're still at work. I guess you'll always be at work. Nothing is happening in my day, but don't worry, I'll comfort myself with my thoughts.

The saddest part of it is that I can predict what's going to happen when you get home tonight. You will be tired. You will leave your briefcase on the table and get into your pajamas. You will lie down on the sofa and watch TV until you fall asleep as you always do, like I'm not even here. You will sleep peacefully and forget that you have a wife who waited for you for too long to make her happy.

Yours,
    Margot

    P.S. When I wore that swimsuit on the beach a few people came up to me and asked me where I bought it. They said I looked lovely. You never complimented me Arthur.

CHAPTER THREE

August 8, 2019

My dear Arthur,

You are like an alien with extraordinary senses. You seem to have sniffed out that I want to escape from this life, so you deliberately put a slice of happiness on the plate to confuse me. What you don't realize is that I've been suffocating from pure sadness for a long time, so you won't succeed Arthur.

You came to me again this morning before you went to work and kissed me on my forehead. My eyes were closed but I was awake. I could feel your energy and I sensed you wanted to tell me something. I guess I know you that well.

"A nice Japanese restaurant just opened here in Trocadero," you said, "would you like to go? We could have dinner there tonight," you whispered to me so gently, as if you really love me. I listened to you, but I didn't say anything.

"Margot dear, can you hear me?"

"Yes, I hear you. I'm just tired Arthur, I don't feel like talking," I said, as I turned around to face the other side.

"Can you be ready at about eight o'clock? I'll be home around that time," you said stroking my hair, and then you left.

As soon as I heard you go out I got up. I felt anxious. Today was supposed to be the day I took my bag and walked out the door, putting this life behind me. Today was supposed to be the day I would stop looking back. You Arthur, look at the power you possess. You destroy things you don't even know about. You destroy my plans for freedom. You're a monster Arthur, you're an absolute monster.

I decided to go with you to see if there was still any spark between us. I was hopeful. I didn't understand why you invited me to dinner when we haven't been anywhere together in months. Your sudden interest in me, your kindness - seemed strange.

I stood in my closet looking at all my clothes, trying to pick an outfit for our date. 'I really have a lot of clothes,'I thought. 'What is the point? I don't go anywhere and I have no opportunity to wear any of these.' You always tell me that I can buy whatever I want to, but what value does the most expensive wardrobe have if the person wearing the clothes is unhappy.

I threw my dresses on the floor because I didn't like any of them. I tried to put on a skirt but it barely fit me. I've put on some weight and it makes me feel ugly. It's all the stress Arthur, it's because of you.

After some rummaging I found a bigger sized dress that I'd never worn. I tried it on and looked at myself in the mirror. I didn't feel sick looking at myself, and that was as much as I could ask for. I decided to wear it.

The time today seemed to slip through my hands. I took a shower and when I checked my watch it was already seven o'clock in the evening. I put on some make-up and braided my hair,then I went to wait for you in the living room. I felt so sad. I had to pinch myself to believe we were actually going out together, but I also knew this was only one day out of the life we share. I waited for you, knowing that I would have to continue with my plan tomorrow.

"Margot, I'm home. Are you ready?"

"Yes," I was sitting on the sofa in the living room, feeling quite nervous.

"I'm just going to change and then we're leaving," you said, going upstairs to the bedroom. You were smiling and I wanted to smile at you too, but I just didn't feel like I could.

I anxiously scratched the arm of the sofa with my fingernails while waiting for you to get ready. Tension engulfed me.

"Ready to go?"

You appeared on the stairs and came toward me.

"Let's go," I said, and got up.

"I'm not telling you that you're beautiful, I know you know that already," you said as you headed for the door. I looked at you in amazement.

During the drive to the restaurant I stared out of the car window. It was a nice evening out, a beautiful summer Paris sky hung over us. 'Paris is a beautiful city,' I thought, 'but why am I so unhappy in Paris then?' I sank into myself forgetting the beauty around me. I drifted away.

At the restaurant I felt uneasy. I hadn't been out for a long time and I swear I had forgotten how to behave. You gave me your hand and we walked into Kura like a fairytale couple. Everything was perfect except that my heart felt like an icy tundra where there might have been life once, but now there was nothing.

The evening ended as I expected. You took out your phone and stared at the screen most of the night. I wanted you to look at me and ask me how I've been, how I've really been, but we barely exchanged any words.You didn't even notice that I had my head held down most of the time, hiding my face in my plate of salmon sashimi, sipping my glass of wine as if I was dining alone. The waiter came over and asked if I needed anything and I felt so self-conscious. I thought it must be so obvious how awkward we were together. I felt like something was wrong with me.

I saw a couple holding hands across the table beside us. They were feeding each other edamame and giggling playfully. On the other side of the room a man gave a woman a kiss on the cheek. Everyone around us seemed happy and relaxed, eating, talking, enjoying themselves, and that made me feel even worse. The funny thing is that you have a way of making me feel guilty for being sad - as if sadness was a sin. I didn't do this

Arthur. I am the victim here. Don't you think I want us to be like these people? Don't you think I want to be happy too? I do, but I'm powerless. When you asked for the bill, I was relieved the date was over. It was like a punishment to see everybody so in love while we were so distant from each other.

When we got home you fell asleep in the living room immediately. I envy you. Every day you are tired of life and every day I am tired of not having a life. That is the huge difference between us, Arthur.

As I'm writing this I'm sitting on the stairs of our picture-perfect house in one of the nicest suburbs in Paris.

I look around and see our original artwork decorating our cream-painted walls, our designer kitchen, the custom-made curtains on the windows overlooking our lovely garden, and then I see you, my handsome husband, oblivious to me, his oh-so-beautiful wife. I'm watching you as you sleep like a log on the sofa in the living room. Your dark brown hair is all messy and you're hugging the pillow like you once used to hug me. I remember when we bought that sofa. We talked about how we'd spend late nights on it, music playing in the background, maybe a fireplace on if it was chilly, just the two of us under a warm blanket watching romantic movies - the classics I like, cuddling and eating popcorn. We talked about how you would watch *The Umbrellas of Cherbourg* with me. You used to know it was my favorite movie. It never happened. I don't know why. I'm almost sure neither of us ever suggested it. I wanted to do those things with you but I thought you didn't want to. I don't know if you thought about suggesting it to me but you never did, so I guess if you wanted it - you didn't want it enough.

You seem to have forgotten so many things about me. All I ever wanted was for you to hold me and for us to talk about everything under the stars.

Yours,
Margot

P.S. I really don't know how you can think I know I'm beautiful. You're wrong Arthur, I don't know I'm beautiful at all, and since my husband never tells me I'm almost positive that I'm not beautiful. Don't you know that about me?

CHAPTER FOUR

August 9, 2019

My dear Arthur,

I knew that today would not be the day I leave you. I'm closer to being ready to do it, I am - or am I further away from it than I ever was before? I don't know my own heart. Arthur, you make me feel so insecure. If only you could feel my sadness and truly know how much I'm suffering.

I slept until noon because I felt numb. I didn't even know what time you left for work. When I opened my eyes it was late and I felt dazed and disoriented. I stood by the bedroom window and stared out past the trees in the garden. I saw our neighbour Mrs. Dupont watering her roses, felt the sunlight streaming in as I drew the curtains, and heard the noise of traffic nearby. I miss the beautiful sunny days I used to enjoy. Now I'm simply too drained to go out and do anything. My sadness has taken away so much from me. I forgot how it feels to wake up and be normal.

I covered my face with the bed linen and just wanted to stay hidden there forever. It seemed I was more lost than ever and all my plans were falling apart. I'm going through all the motions of daily life but I'm not living. I needed to talk and I had no one else to call, so I called you, Arthur.

"Yes, Margot," you said. I was happy when I heard your voice.

"Arthur?"

"Yes, Margot, I'm listening to you." You were so self-assured, and I was such a basket case.

I couldn't remember exactly why I called you in the first place, so I said nothing. I just held the phone to my ear, trembling with anxiety.

"Margot, I'm with people. You're not saying anything," you said. I remained silent. "See you later, okay? I love you Margot," you said and hung up.

I drew the curtains because all of a sudden, I couldn't stand the sun. I threw myself on our bedroom floor and started crying.

"How could you say that you love me, Arthur? I don't believe you. Why do you tell me such lies? Why can't you let me have my sadness? Isn't it enough that you've already taken away all my joy? Why Arthur, why?"

I screamed these things out loud and heard my voice echo through the room. I was filled with despair. You're killing me Arthur, giving me enough hope to be half-alive, just alive enough to suffer.

I sprawled my body across the carpet, motionless for an entire hour. I couldn't get up. My skin felt like it didn't fit me. I wanted to disappear and run away from everything. I thought I might lose my mind any second, but I had no choice but to pull myself together. Slowly, I got up. I decided to take a shower.

The water felt good on my skin, it helped me relax. When I got out of the shower, I looked into the bathroom mirror. It was fogged up so I wiped it clear with my hand to see my reflection. I forced a smile and felt a bit better. The desire to make myself look pretty came over me. I fixed my hair and my make-up, and put on some red lipstick so that I could feel sexy. I remembered how you always told me that red lipstick suited my long ginger hair and complemented my green eyes. That was the biggest compliment you ever gave me, and anyway - I didn't only want compliments about how I looked. I put on one of my favorite white skirts and a matching shirt that I knew I used to look good in. I always liked myself in white. The innocence of the color masked my internal sadness.

I flipped through my clothes hanging in the closet and saw my bag, the one that I kept ready and waiting for the moment

I worked up enough nerve to leave. I picked it up and opened it. It was still filled with all the blouses, skirts, and pants that I had packed in. It made me feel angry. I was angry at myself for falling for your words so easily. One random bit of kindness from your lips, and I doubt my heart, my plans, and I get caught up between pain and hope. You lead me on and then never follow through with any concrete changes, but you won't play me this time Arthur.My loneliness is bigger than your insincerity.

That evening when you got home, I was watching TV and you saw that I was all dressed up.You gave me a strange look and then a wry little smile. I saw it but I pretended I didn't. You were mocking me Arthur. You thought I was a fool.

"Did you need me today, Margot?"

"No," I said, seething because you weren't aware that I needed you all the time.

"Alright, I'll go to bed then, I'm very tired," you said and went into the bedroom. You came back into the living room a few moments later in your pajamas and sat on the sofa next to me. You clicked the TV remote, changing the channel without even asking me. I said nothing, I got up and went into the bedroom.

As I'm writing this letter you're lost in your dreams for the night, hugging your pillow down in the living room. I can't sleep. I want to stay awake and be dressed up like this for as long as possible, like I'm the same Margot I once was, alluring and happy.

Yours,
  Margot

P.S. When you got home today, for a few moments we were like two people seeing each other for the first time, two people who are attracted to each other. In those few seconds I forgot all the reasons why we're not happy.

CHAPTER FIVE

August 10, 2019

My dear Arthur,

I was half-awake this morning when I heard your voice.

"Margot? Margot? Can you hear me? Margot, Michaela is coming back from Romania today. Don't forget," you said, and kissed me on the forehead before you left.

I woke up as you spoke to me, but I didn't open my eyes for the next ten minutes. Michaela! I had completely forgotten about Michaela! She had reminded me that she was coming back from Romania on the tenth of August so many times.

I worried that she would notice how unhappy I was. She's a good housekeeper, but also very perceptive and reads my energy well - that makes me nervous around her. At one point I thought of confessing our marital problems to Michaela. I considered telling her that you don't even touch me anymore. I thought she might understand how I felt, woman to woman, but I decided I didn't want to open up about my deepest vulnerabilities to someone who works for us. She probably couldn't relate to what I was going through anyway. She's not married after all, and besides, she has her own problems with her mother back home. I didn't want to burden her.

Even with Michaela coming back to work today, my plan to leave was still in place - only postponed to another day, yet again. I would have to be here to get her settled in. I left my bag with the clothes and essentials I'd need if I left, in the closet. If Michaela found it while cleaning my room I would be found out, so I decided I would simply tell her I was rearranging my wardrobe and I didn't want her to touch anything in my closet until I was finished.

I took a shower to release my anxiety. Hot water streamed over my body, pulsating against my skin. I ran my hands through my hair until I was soaked all over. I could feel each drop on my skin, soothing me. In that moment my world seemed at peace, transporting me from my reality. I wanted to keep that feeling so I stayed in the shower for a while.

As I rinsed the soap off my skin, I heard Michaela's voice and it brought me back to the present.

"Mrs. Margot, I'm back. Mrs. Margot, are you in the bathroom? I'm downstairs in the living room," she called out. She must have heard the water running.

"I'll be down in a minute," I said as loud as I could, already starting to plan every word I would say to her.

Michaela has always had an effect on me. I don't know why Arthur, but sometimes I think you didn't hire her to help me in our home, but to make me feel useless instead. Every time she looks at me, she looks at me with disappointment. I have a feeling that Michaela pities me and I can't blame her for that. I am pitied Arthur, that was your goal, wasn't it?

With a fake smile on my face, I stepped out of the bathroom, tying my bathrobe around my waist. I went downstairs to the living room and there she was, Michaela. She had already started dusting the mantelpiece, her usual efficient self.

"Mrs. Margot, how are you?"

She smiled and came over to hug me.

"Michaela," I said, "I'm fine, how are you? How was Romania?" I could barely hug her back.

"Okay, Lassi is the same as always. As you leave it, so you will find it, but I saw my mother and that was important to me."

"Yes, yes," I sighed. "How is she, your mother?"

"She's ok, she's still working at the hospital. Five more

years and she'll retire. I think what keeps her going is that she really loves her job, she wants to be a nurse, she enjoys helping people."

I smiled. "I understand," I said. "My mother worked in a factory in the textile industry her whole life. She loved her job very much, although I think she struggled a lot. After my father died, it was even harder, but she didn't give up. She went to work smiling every day and always had hope. She's retired now, for almost four years. She's home alone, and never complains, but I know it's not easy for her. Life is hard," I said. The words seemed to be pouring out of me.

"Mrs. Eliza, yes, I remember her, even though I've only met her once. A strong woman, an amazing woman. Ah, Mrs. Margot, but life isn't hard, life is very beautiful, it's so beautiful! We should celebrate life every day," she said, looking at me.

I didn't say anything.

"Alright, Mrs. Margot, I have a lot of work to do. If you need anything, just let me know," she said, and went on dusting the mantelpiece.

I went upstairs to the bedroom feeling worthless, miserable, and sick of myself. I always feel that way after talking to Michaela. She doesn't have a clue of course, she lives in her own small world and dares to talk about life as if she understands it. No wonder she is so plain-looking. She doesn't understand anything, that's why she allows herself to think such foolish things. Life is beautiful, indeed! Life is sad, ugly, and incredibly torturous. That is my life. Either Michaela is completely unaware of the reality of what is happening in the world, or unfortunately she lives with limited senses and limited intelligence which prevents her from understanding reality. What a horror!

Around five in the afternoon you came home, all smiling and cheerful. For me the day had passed more quickly than I expected. It normally drags.

"Hey there," you said coming in. I was having a lie-down on

the sofa, staring at the TV blankly.

"Hello," I replied.

"Margot, where is Michaela?"

"I said she could leave early today. I thought she should take a break since she must be tired from traveling," I changed the TV channels as I spoke, trying to look casual and hide my anxiety.

"Is that so?"

"What does that mean?" I asked. My voice was tense.

You didn't answer me, you walked upstairs trying to avoid the conversation.

"Arthur!" I screamed.

You turned around, came toward me, and raising your voice you asked, "What was it today Margot?"

"Why are you treating me like this?" I replied, and tears came flooding down my cheeks.

"And what about you - why are *you* treating me like this? Why, Margot? And why are you treating yourself like this? Do you even know why?"

Your voice was loud and angry so I said nothing further. I just wanted it to be quiet. You left the living room and locked yourself in the bedroom. I stayed downstairs for hours, sitting on the sofa, pacing, trying to find peace. Finally, I started writing this letter late at night, you must have been asleep already.

It turned out that I was the one who was going to sleep in the living room tonight, and that was the only thing that the fight changed between us - our sleeping arrangements. I've seen you sleep in the living room so comfortably night after night, I didn't even think about sleeping in our guest bedroom either. I can't handle another big, empty bed. Everything is in vain. There are no happy people here Arthur. I'm not happy, you're not happy, but I'm devastated about this marriage failing, and you - you can obviously live with it.

Yours,

Margot

P.S. When you asked me why I treated you like that, I had a clear answer. When you asked me why I treated myself like that, I didn't know what to say. Do you see Arthur? I am completely lost.

CHAPTER SIX

August 11, 2019

My dear Arthur,

I couldn't sleep again tonight. I tossed and turned, rolling over on the sofa from side to side, while you must have slept like a log in the bedroom upstairs. Our bed is not for a married couple, that bed is a place of separation, a place full of sorrow and incredible silence.

I was not feeling well at all Arthur. I could hardly breathe. I couldn't stand it. I wanted to die Arthur.

This morning I woke up to the noise of Michaela around the house. My entire body hurt and my soul was exhausted. She was in the kitchen most of the day. She made me some tea and she vacuumed. I couldn't swallow anything, I hid in the bedroom and felt dejected. Lying down on the bed, I could smell you everywhere.

Michaela came into the bedroom with chamomile tea and tried to get me to speak to her.

"Mrs. Margot?"

I didn't reply, I just turned to the other side.

"I will leave the tea here, please drink it, it will make you feel better," she said putting the tea down. I remained quiet, but she didn't give up.

"Mrs. Margot, come downstairs and watch some TV. I'll prepare some vegetable soup and we can talk." She never spoke to me like that before. She was always professional and kept her fair distance. It was obvious she felt sorry for me.

"Mrs. Margot ..."

She was so persistent I had to relent.

"Alright, Michaela, alright. Let me get dressed and I'll come downstairs," I gave in, hoping that as soon as I went downstairs she would shut up and let me stare at the TV.

It took me half an hour to leave the room and as I came downstairs I could smell the soup cooking on the stove. Michaela cooks very well. I used to cook too, but in this marriage you and I barely see each other Arthur, so I have no reason to cook. I sat on the sofa and turned on the TV.

"Mrs. Margot, when are you going to cook again? Mr. Arthur always says you cook such nice dishes."

"Really? I haven't heard him say such a thing."

"Yes, he said that when you met you made him the most divine spaghetti bolognaise, and after that spaghetti, no other spaghetti was good enough," laughed Michaela.

I completely forgot about it, Arthur. It's true, isn't it? I used to make the most delicious spaghetti that you couldn't get enough of. Once jokingly, after eating three helpings, you put your arms around my waist and kissed the top of my head and said you only married me because of my spaghetti. We were happy then, weren't we?

Michaela came to sit down beside me and said, "Mrs. Margot, tomorrow is your wedding anniversary, right? Why not surprise Mr. Arthur and make him your famous spaghetti? He won't be expecting that and it'll make him happy," she smiled, not knowing that she was striking me where it hurt the most.

"Why do you think he won't expect it? What do you mean by that? Are you saying that I don't do anything all day and that's why my husband doesn't expect me to be able to make him an ordinary plate of spaghetti?"

I was furious. I shook as I got up from the sofa.

"Mrs. Margot, please forgive me," Michaela began to cry. I just couldn't look at her like that so I ran upstairs and locked myself in the bedroom.

I started screaming, breaking everything I could get my hands on, plucking at my hair, scratching and hurting myself. I was frantic and lost control. Michaela knocked at the door but I didn't open it.

"Damn you, Arthur," I screamed out loud."Why do you get to me like this?"

I didn't care if Michaela could hear me,or what she would think.

I stopped crying after two hours and went downstairs. Michaela was in the living room.

"Are you still here?"

"Yes, I had some more work to finish," she said.

"Don't lie to me. I know you stayed because you're afraid to leave me alone."

"That too," she nodded, and I knew I should apologize.

"Michaela, I'm sorry, it's not your fault. I'm going through something, it's complicated. I'm sorry. I didn't intend to hurt you," I said, approaching her.

"I'm not angry Mrs. Margot, I'm just worried about you."

I smiled and sat down on the sofa. I started to watch some stupid movie so that I could stop thinking about what had happened for a second. Michaela didn't say another word to me, which was exactly what I wanted. After a couple of hours you came home Arthur, and Michaela was getting ready to leave. It was clear that she was babysitting me. I was surprised to see that she respected my privacy enough not to say a word about my outburst to you. When you asked her how her day was, she said it was great. Maybe Michaela understands me more than I thought.

"Hello Margot," you said when you saw me watching TV.

"Hello Arthur," I replied.

"How are you?"

I shrugged without answering.You came toward me and must have noticed my eyes were swollen from crying, but you didn't say anything.

"Okay," you said, "I'm tired. I'm going upstairs," and you turned to leave the room.

I was still silent and you turned around suddenly to look at me, saying, "Margot, tomorrow..."

My heart skipped a beat.

"Yes," I said. "What is it?"

I thought you might remember, but at the same time I was doubtful that you cared at all.

"Tomorrow is Monday, right?"

"Yes," I said, confirming with a nod of my head, like a robot.

"I don't know what day it is anymore. That's how it is when you work all the time," you said, smiling and going upstairs to the bedroom without saying anything else.

Idiot, you're the biggest idiot, Arthur. I don't even know how I could have thought you'd remember that tomorrow is our anniversary. You'll see, tomorrow I'll surprise you. I'll surprise you by running away from this unhappiness.

My day ended with this letter, with incredible silence, and a closed door - a door behind which a stranger is sleeping on a half-empty bed, a stranger who is in fact my husband.

Yours,
    Margot

P.S. When Michaela suggested I make your favorite spaghetti and surprise you for our anniversary, for a moment I thought it was a good idea. Even for a moment, I was able to imagine the two of us at home sitting at the dining room table where we almost never sat, eating spaghetti, talking, laughing, and enjoying each other's company as if nothing was as difficult as it seems to be.

CHAPTER SEVEN

August 12, 2019

My dear Arthur,

When I opened my eyes there was a red rose on the living room table. It was breathtaking. There was a card beside it, and inside you had written a few words:

If I could turn back time- I wouldn't change a thing.
Happy anniversary, my Margot!

With love,
Arthur.

Arthur, why are you doing this to me? Why are you deliberately hurting me? You haven't forgotten our anniversary but yesterday you acted as if you didn't remember it at all. It seems like you know when I might expect something from you, and then you deliberately don't give it to me. Why are you doing that? Do you want me to go crazy?

I got up from the sofa with the rose in my hand and saw Michaela coming in through the front door.

"Michaela, fill a vase with water and put a teaspoon of sugar in it, please. I'm just going upstairs to take a shower and get ready, then I'll come to make some spaghetti."

Michaela smiled and I smiled back at her.

I stepped into the bathroom and looked at myself in the mirror. I stared at my reflection and questioned how I felt. It was wonderful that you did something nice for once, but that doesn't automatically mean everything is alright and that I'm happy. It doesn't mean that everything is forgotten and that my plan ends here. No! I can't forget the nights I cried myself to sleep, the anger, and the pain. I don't think I will ever stop feeling the ache you caused.

After taking a shower I turned on the faucet in the basin and washed my face. I tried not to think of us. I reached for my jar of eye cream from the bathroom cabinet and pulled out a thick clump of creamy moisturizer. I smoothed it over the soft areas under my eyes. 'I haven't taken care of my face in a long time,' I thought. When a woman is unhappy she has no desire to do anything. I've been letting myself go Arthur, and you are to blame for that.

I wrapped my robe around me and opened my closet, picking out my favorite red dress to wear for you that evening. It chose a silk dress that fell just below my knee. It felt soft on my skin. I liked the scarlet because it's red like the rose you gave me. I wish I could say that the dress was red like our love, but that would be a lie.

"Michaela, I'm coming," I shouted, coming downstairs with the rose in my hand, like I was a woman full of self-confidence.

"Mrs. Margot, you look beautiful today," Michaela said, trying to flatter me. "Give me the rose, let me put it in a vase for you."

She took the rose and put it in the sugar water that I had asked her to prepare earlier, "Wow," she said, straightening it in the vase, "it's so beautiful."

"Michaela, you're just being silly," I said, "I don't look any different today than I do on other days."

I sat down on the barstool in the kitchen and tried to hide the smile on my face.

"No, really, you're glowing," she smiled at me. "I think it's because today is your anniversary, am I right?"

"Yes, we know what day it is," I said bluntly. "Instead of being silly, I suggest you help me make my famous spaghetti,

I think I've forgotten how to make it," I added a little shyly.

Michaela smiled sweetly and started taking out some ingredients.

"Mrs. Margot, do you know what?"

"What?"

"You haven't forgotten, you just need to refresh your memory," she said, encouraging me. I didn't answer her - I just started preparing the ingredients.

As I washed the pasta, I realized how long it had been since I prepared anything in my own kitchen.That made me feel incredibly sad.

"This big, beautiful kitchen seems like such a waste," I said, looking at Michaela. "Arthur and I don't cook, we never sit here together, we used it a little bit in the beginning but that's it, we just don't use it anymore."

"Yes I know, but that's up to you," she said as she sliced the vegetables.

"What do you mean?"

"Well, no one is stopping you from using it. I mean, if you want to you have everything you need right here. If you decide to eat at home and have dinner together, you can do that anytime." The truth of her words annoyed me.

"Yes, but I have no motivation, Michaela. Arthur is constantly at work and when he comes home he goes to bed immediately because he's tired. He often eats before he even gets here and I grab a quick bite.I eat alone, most likely something that you prepared for me," I said.

"Yes, but that can be changed. Maybe Mr. Arthur eats out because he's used to it."

I listened to the point she made, but thought that whatever I do, it would never be enough for you Arthur. That's where the problem begins. My every effort is not enough for you.

"It looks great," Michaela smiled.

"Yes," I smiled back, and then I suddenly said, "Michaela, go upstairs to the bedroom, tidy up there please, I don't need you here anymore."

"Are we done?" She gave me a perplexed look.

"No, but I'm going to make the sauce myself, I can handle it from here," I said, sliding my fingers through the cooked spaghetti.

"Ok, great," she said with a surprised tone and went upstairs, smiling. I know she thought she motivated me and that thanks to her words I made an effort, but she doesn't realize it's all in vain. Michaela doesn't know you Arthur. She thinks of you as a poor, hard-working businessman who has to eat out because his wife doesn't cook for him at home. She doesn't know how cruel you can be or how much you can ruin my desire to do something nice for you. Anyone would get tired and I'm not any different. I got tired and stopped trying. It was as if someone tied my hands, closed my eyes, closed my mouth, and shouted at me, 'Live, live as before!'

After I prepared dinner for the two of us, I completely forgot about all the anger I had inside me. For just a moment, I felt like a real woman, with a real husband, and a real life. Michaela left and I went upstairs to get ready. I took my time, not rushing. I showered slowly, styled my hair, put on the red dress I'd picked out earlier, and put on some make-up. I looked in the mirror and really believed I hadn't been this beautiful in a long time. I saw the old me in the mirror's reflection and it made me happy, but it was a mixed joy, mixed with sadness, tainted by a feeling that happiness doesn't really exist, not purely. Arthur, I feel like I'm in some space shuttle which no human has ever been in before. I'm on my own and I have no instructions, just an awareness that I'm heading down an abyss. Driving it is fun at times, even beautiful, but that doesn't change the fact that I'm falling.

I dabbed some perfume on the inside of my elbows. I chose the Guerlain in the pink bottle that you bought for my birthday, and then I was completely ready. I went downstairs and started setting the table, expecting you to come in at any moment. We didn't speak to each other at all today. I deliberately didn't call you because I wanted all of this to be a surprise.

As I lit the candles, I heard you open the door.

"Margot, are you here?"

I wondered if perhaps you thought no one was home because the lights were switched off, only the candles were flickering.

"Yes," I called to you, and listened to your footsteps slowly moving toward the kitchen.

"Margot? Margot, what's going on? You look different," you said."You look pretty, your dress is beautiful. I think I've only seen you wear it once before," you smiled, and I could see you were disarmed. "What's all this?" First you looked at me, then you looked at the table, and all around. You seemed pleasantly surprised.

"This is dinner for us, for our anniversary. I wanted to do something nice for you. I wanted to surprise you," I said.

"I'm surprised alright," you said, "I didn't expect this at all,including the dim lights." Your eyes flittered across the room taking it all in, and then you saw the rose you had left me, tall in the vase.

"Did you like the rose?"

"Yes I did, thank you," I smiled. "Shall we sit down?" I felt nervous.

"Let's sit down," you said. "Just give me a few minutes, I want to change and clean up a bit."

I watched you go upstairs with loving eyes, you were the man I fell madly in love with. Our years together passed through my mind like a movie, as if we were standing at the very beginning when we first met, and everything was different. I wanted to go back to the time when we loved each other, when that was enough.

When you came back down you were in a plain white t-shirt and gray athletic pants.

"I haven't seen you like this in a long time."

"Like this?"

You took a seat at the table and looked down at what you were wearing.

"I see you either in a suit or in your pajamas," I smiled.

"Yes. I'm in work clothes all the time,and when I come home I'm tired and get straight into my pj's. I didn't want to have dinner in my pajamas though, but I wanted to be comfortable," you said. "You on the other hand are all dressed up. I hope I'm not embarrassing you by saying that" you smiled at me.

I returned your smile. "It's perfectly alright. Don't worry about it," I said, "Shall we start?"

"Let's. I'm famished."

I put the spaghetti on the table and served the salad I made as a starter.

"For dessert, I have a surprise!"

"Margot, my favorite spaghetti," you said. "I thought I would never eat this again!"

"Why?" I asked, feeling offended by the comment.

"It doesn't matter, let's change the subject. "Wine?"

"Yes, wine please."

You got up to get some wine and I tried to hide how nervous I felt.

"Margot, I have to tell you, you really caught me off guard." You raised your glass and made a toast, "Cheers!"

"Cheers, Arthur. And you caught me off guard too."

"I did?"

You dished spaghetti and salad at the same time, and I found myself staring at your plate. I had expected us to eat the salad first and the spaghetti as the main course. The way you dished up was a small thing, but I let it bother me.

"Yes," I said, trying not to let my irritation show, "you surprised me with the rose this morning."

"The rose I left for you?" You began to eat and said, "It needs a little salt," then reached for the salt shaker.

"You don't usually eat very salty food," I said.

"I never used to eat very salty food, but recently I've started liking it."

It sounded to me like you said that with a sarcastic tone, so I asked, "What is that supposed to mean?"

"It doesn't mean anything except that I didn't eat salty food before, and now I do."

"Damn you!" I screamed, getting up from the table. "Do you think I'm an idiot and I don't understand anything? You're implying that I don't know you anymore, that you're not the same person you were, and that I don't even realize it! You're implying that I'm stuck in the past, right?"

"Margot, don't do this, please," you continued, trying to diffuse my anger.

"No, Arthur! I didn't do this, you did it. I knew it would be like this. I knew it. That's why I don't bother, that's why my every hope for us has died. That's why - because you are incredibly cruel Arthur, because you are evil." I started crying, and in a fit of tears I got up and left the table.

"Margot, why do you have to destroy everything?"

You reached for my hand but I pushed you away. Through my tears I said, "You destroyed me. Don't you see? Don't you see that?" I couldn't calm down. "Please leave me alone. I want to pretend this isn't happening. Just leave me," I said. I ran upstairs trembling, and locked myself in the bedroom.

It is almost midnight now and I'm writing this while I'm locked in the bedroom. I can't stop crying, Arthur. I can't calm down. My hands are shaking and I can barely hold the pen. My whole body aches. My soul is sick, Arthur. You took my soul and threw it into a black hole.

Yours,

Margot

P.S. You may not believe me, but tonight something different could have happened, something that hasn't happened for a long time. Tonight, at least for a while, you and I could've been you and I again.

CHAPTER EIGHT

August 13, 2019

My dear Arthur,

I don't know what's happening to me today, I have no strength at all. After the dismal failure of our romantic dinner I realized that all my darkest thoughts were real. You really do hate me, and I can't put up with it any longer. I don't want this life anymore, not even for one more day. I don't want this unrest that lingers in me, nor do I want this sadness that doesn't let me out of its dungeon.

Did you know I slept for almost twelve hours last night? When I woke up this morning I heard Michaela downstairs. I thought I should go have some coffee at least, but I didn't have the strength to get dressed. I just wrapped myself in a bathrobe and went into the kitchen.

"Mrs. Margot, there you are," Michaela smiled at me.

"Yes, here I am," I smiled back, not hiding my cynicism. "Michaela, I don't feel great today, let me warn you," I said right away.

"I can tell," she nodded.

"I didn't know it was that obvious."

"Yes, when I came in this morning everything was left like it was last night. The food was barely eaten at all, so I assumed something went wrong."

"Yes, you're right," I looked down. "Michaela, your idea of making spaghetti for him didn't work well."

"Why? What happened? Wasn't the spaghetti good?" She looked at me concerned, and I couldn't decide if she was being deliberately naive or simply didn't understand me.

"No, the spaghetti was fine, but all of my effort was for nothing."

"Mrs. Margot, I'm really sorry. I don't know what happened, but I'm really sorry," she came up to me and hugged me. I started crying uncontrollably.

"I'll leave him, Michaela. I will leave that cruel, horrible man," I said in a loud outburst, sinking into Michaela's arms.

"Calm down, Mrs. Margot, please calm down," she said.

"I can't, Michaela,I can't do it anymore!"

"This will pass, it will pass, Mrs. Margot."

"My life is over, my life is over!"

"Mrs. Margot, calm down, please. I want to tell you something, it might make you feel better." She wiped my tears with her t-shirt. "Come on, I'll make you a cup of coffee, it'll do you good. We'll have coffee together and I'll tell you my story, can I?"

I nodded, feeling terrible.

Michaela poured me some coffee and I took deep breaths. My eyes were focused on one spot, transfixed like I was empty inside. I felt my body and soul separate from each other. I couldn't find my center.

"There you go," Michaela said, handing me the cup. It smelled really good, but I couldn't appreciate it. I realized I had lost my ability to find happiness in small things. It used to be my best trait. In the past, small things made me so happy. I noticed everything and appreciated every moment, I was able to see all the beauty that life offered.

"Michaela, before you start, can I ask you something?"

"Of course, of course," she said.

"Do you believe that it's possible to lose yourself completely and then find yourself again?"

"Mrs. Margot if you get lost, you can come back better," she smiled at me.

"Do you really believe that?"

"Absolutely, Mrs. Margot."

I sighed.

"Mrs. Margot, I'm thirty-five years old and I can't have children. I've known that for eight years, and I live with it. I had an inflammatory disease of the small pelvis. When they removed my uterus it was as if they removed my heart. I was dead, but still alive. My father died the same year. My mother was in a terrible mental state and I was trying to be strong for both of us, even though I didn't have any strength, not even for myself. After many days of grief, tears, and pain, one day I just couldn't do it anymore. I couldn't. I didn't want to live like that for another single day. I didn't want to be sad anymore, to be angry. I was disgusted with myself, so I decided to change my life and I moved to Paris to start over. I quit my job as a high school English teacher. My mother thought I was crazy and selfish. 'How can you go to Paris, broken-hearted, and leave me here alone?' she asked. I'll never forget her words. 'I'm going to get well, Mom,' I said. 'We're all, each of us, alone in this world, and we have to face it. I'm always here for you, but I can't live my life for you.'

She was angry at me for a while, but then she understood what I was trying to tell her. I wasn't even sure what I was doing, but I knew I had to take my life into my own hands. When I came to Paris I was lost, scared, and sad. I didn't know where to begin. I didn't know anything, but I didn't give up. I started to love Paris. I fell in love with every day and with my life - exactly as it was. I stopped focusing on things I didn't have. I began to believe in myself, to look forward to every moment, to learn to be happy.

It wasn't easy, every day meant hard work. At first I couldn't find a job, but I didn't allow that to drag me down. I strongly believed that something good would happen for me, that I'd find my way and my light. When I felt like crying I would go out and walk, and all the beauty around me would give me reasons to laugh. One day I found your job advertisement.

Although I have a university degree I knew that in Paris I was a different person, and that I shouldn't be guided by who and what I'd been in Romania. That's why I applied for this job, to broaden my horizons, to show me new colors of life, and to give me new energy. We can never know what kind of people we'll meet in life, and what things and lessons we'll learn from them. When you hired me I was overjoyed. It meant a dependable salary, a nice place to live, and a stable life. I devoted myself completely to my new job and learned to love it. Then I realized that all those people who quit jobs that they find unfulfilling aren't heroes at all, but cowards. A hero is someone who manages to find something beautiful in whatever job they have. I was trying to be my own hero. I was trying to be a better version of myself every day, to be proud of who I am, to discover and learn new things, and only then did doors open for me. Apart from this job, I started tutoring. I gave private English lessons, but that would never have happened if I hadn't had this job, because I met those people through you. One opportunity led me to another, and with time my story was woven together. If I had stayed stuck between four walls I would have remained entangled in my own problems. Nothing happens for people who don't want anything to happen for them. Absolutely everything is a personal choice Mrs. Margot, and most of all sadness and happiness. I chose to be a happy person and although I had a million reasons to cry, I chose to laugh."

Michaela's speech left me dumbfounded. I really didn't know what to say. It seems I was so arrogant and superficial that I failed to see there was someone in my own home that I could learn a lot from.I thought of my mother for a moment, unable to ignore the difference between her and Michaela's mother. My mother never asked me to stay by her side, the only thing she wanted for me was to be honest with myself and have my own life. When I told her I was going to move to Paris she was overjoyed, and although she was left all alone she said,

'Go, my child, go and live your life!'

"And love, Michaela?" I asked.

"Love starts with ourselves," she said. "The biggest love in life exists when we are fully happy with who we are. I'm very close to achieving that, Mrs. Margot," she smiled at me.

"And I'm so far away from it," I lowered my head.

"That will change," she said, looking at me.

I was silent.

"Mrs. Margot, I'm going to tidy up the garden a little, okay? I'm sorry if I talked to you for too long," she said, perhaps thinking that my silence meant I simply had nothing more to say.

"No no. Thank you. I'm sorry, dear Michaela," I replied.

"Sorry? For what?"

"For everything," I answered, and looked up at her, then headed to the bedroom. As I was climbing the stairs I sighed hard a few times. A strange kind of relief came over me.

I entered my room and looked at my closet. I opened it, knelt down, and took out the bag hidden behind the dresses. I looked at it and felt absolutely nothing. I sighed again. I noticed how untidy the cupboard was and felt an overwhelming need to clean it out. We had so many clothes that we didn't need, it was just cluttering up the place and I thought it looked chaotic.

"It's time," I said out loud.

I didn't even know what I was doing but I knew I had to start doing something. I took each item of clothing off its hanger, opened the drawers and emptied them. Soon there was a huge pile of clothes in the middle of the room. I looked at it, smiled and said loudly, "Piece by piece, turns into a pile. Same goes with grief."

Instead of looking at the pile and falling into despair, I began to sort it out. I took each piece of clothing into my hands, examined it, and decided what to do with it. I was determined, disciplined, and incredibly dedicated. I forgot about time, I forgot about you Arthur, I forgot about everything. I stepped into another world and for the first time in a while I was able to control the situation I found myself in. I began to feel sudden joy, and immediately afterward, not allowing my grief to swallow the little happiness I just felt, I began to believe that there may be some hidden strength inside of me.

I completely lost track of time, and after a whileI heard your footsteps on the stairs.

"Margot, are you here?"

I heard you call out several times, but I didn't answer, I was too engrossed in what I was doing.

"Margot, where are you?"

You came into the bedroom and gave me an astonished look, "Margot, what are you doing? What are you doing with all these clothes?"

"I'm sorting it out, Arthur."

"I see, but why?"

"Because this is a mess and I want to fix it."

"Mess? Do you think this mess can be fixed?"

You leaned against the bedroom door and I raised my head to look at you, I had tears in my eyes that I couldn't hide.

"You will find the solution to your biggest problem right in the heart of your biggest pain," I said.

You took your pajamas and I heard you going downstairs. I just kept sorting out the clothes.

As I write this late at night from our bedroom, my mind is racing and my heart is going a hundred miles an hour. I don't feel bad, I feel excited. I'm slowly beginning to understand some new things, like how much courage it takes to keep doing what you're doing even when you have a million reasons to stop. It requires incredible power. It occurred to me that this was the opposite of what I had been doing and that my behavior represented not strength, but one great weakness.

Yours,
    Margot

P.S. Her words still ring in my head, I can't forget them. They make me think more deeply:

'Absolutely everything is a personal choice, Mrs. Margot, and most of all sadness and happiness.'

CHAPTER NINE

August 14, 2019

My dear Arthur,

You didn't feel well this morning. You may have thought you saw a ghost when you found me still on the bedroom floor, tidying up.

"Margot, didn't you sleep?"

"I slept but I got up very early and continued where I left off."

"Margot, you've changed everything around," you said, as you came closer and looked in the closet.

You were pale.

"Arthur, are you okay?" I asked. I got up and came to you because you looked sick.

"I woke up in the middle of the night feeling a bit queasy, but don't worry, it'll pass," you said, touching your forehead with your hand.

"Do you want me to get you something? Tea, breakfast? Do you want a pill?"

"No, no," you looked at me disoriented. "I'll get something at work."

"Okay," I smiled at you and continued to tidy up. "Arthur?"

"Yes?"

"I've almost sorted out my side completely, I'm going to give these things to someone who needs them, some of it to Michaela, and I'll put some of the clothes in the big metal boxes on the streets. If I put them in the metal boxes, they should reach the people who need them the most. Do you want me to sort out your side as well?"

"No, that's' fine. Margot. Where did all this come from?"

"What do you mean, *this?*"

"I mean this unexpected desire to tidy up the closet. Where does this need to suddenly help, to donate clothes come from?"

I smiled, got up, and walked past you, opening the curtains of our bedroom windows.

"What a beautiful day," I said, and exhaled. "Arthur, if you decide you want to get your closet in order, tell me, okay?" I said, passing you. "Have a nice day," I stopped and kissed you on the cheek, then went into the bathroom.

I felt a great sense of peace slowly entering my soul. I heard you leaving the bedroom, and I looked in the bathroom mirror, smiling at my reflection. I said out loud to my image, 'So the story had a completely different side. The perception of things is the greatest virtue or the greatest flaw a person can have. I'm Margot and I'm a big fool. I thought I was on the right track, I believed that there was always one enemy who was responsible for all my misfortune. In this world full of possibilities, I chose to yearn for another world.There is nothing more frightening than spending your whole life running away from evil, and to allow evil to destroy you because it lingers inside you.'

I stroked my face and let my ginger hair down, noticing that it desperately needed to be washed. 'Margot, you can actually be someone else. In fact, you can be anything you want to be,' I touched my reflection in the mirror. 'How wonderful that is, isn't it? How simple, clear, and precise it is! I never blamed myself before, I never considered that it all came back to me, and I never thought that maybe I should be the one to change and start doing things differently.'

I took a shower and washed my long hair, dried it, and plaited it. I wore comfortable sneakers, one of my favorite white pants and a simple t-shirt. I emptied out the bag which I had been hiding in my closet - that bag represented my ticket to leaving you. I realized this wasn't how the desire to live is packaged. Instead, I filled the bag with the clothes I wanted to give away. I packed in some things for Michaela too. I put her things in a large paper bag.

When I went downstairs with the bag full of clothes Michaela was surprised, she probably thought I was running away or going somewhere.

"Mrs. Margot ..."

"Don't worry, Michaela," I said, "it's not what you think. Yesterday I cleaned out the closet and separated what I wasn't wearing from what I wear. This is for you, I think you'll like it," I handed her the bag.

"Mrs. Margot - you shouldn't, really, you shouldn't. I'm not comfortable taking things from you," she said.

"Michaela, please. I really want the things I don't use to be used by someone. There's more clothes, I'll put them in those big metal boxes on the streets."

"Yes I know those boxes. Okay then, thank you, thank you very much," Michaela smiled.

"I'm going to take the clothes away now, so I'll see you later."

"Mrs. Margot?"

"Yes?" I was already leaving so I turned to face her.

"It's nice what you're doing," she smiled at me.

"Yes," I said, "I think so too."

As I left the house, I was conscious of how long it had been since I was outdoors. Everything felt strange to me, as if I was in Paris for the first time. I considered walking, but because the bag of clothing I had was heavy, I decided to take the car and drive around to find one of the metal boxes. I thought I would take a walk through our neighborhood later. The weather was warm and nice after all.

I found a metal box in Trocadero, not far from our house. I took the clothes out of the bag I had packed it into, one by one, and put it into the box. I left the car there to walk home, and was reminded of how wonderful our neighbourhood is. Sixteenth District is full of museums, shops, and great restaurants. It's one of the most beautiful places to live in Paris, and has an urban, modern feel. We're truly blessed to live here. I had forgotten that.

Walking down our street, I was carried away by euphoria. I smiled and greeted the people I passed. I remembered that today was Wednesday, and on Wednesday's, my favorite market 'President Wilson' was open. I have such good memories of that market, Arthur. When I first came to live in Paris, I went there every Saturday with you, remember? Although that time didn't last long, I remember it well. In my mind I recall beautiful flowers, delicious fruit and vegetables, fresh fish and seafood, meat and cheese, smiling faces and crowds. As I thought back to how it was then, I realized how much I missed it and decided to be spontaneous and go. The market is quite close to our street, only a short distance away, and I was happy to walk there.

I think I arrived in less than a minute. I was greeted by an incredible crowd of people. It's always bustling and almost everything that's sold there is delicious and fresh. I thought I'd follow our old route - first the meat, then the fish, then the seafood, then the fruit and vegetables, then the cheese, and finally the flowers. I walked through the market slowly, looking around and thinking about what I really wanted to buy. I decided not to plan anything, but to simply enjoy the experience as if it was my first time. I was swept away by the intoxicating scent of beautiful irises. I knew I wanted to take them home and put them in a vase in the living room, so I bought a bouquet of pretty blue ones and some fresh fruit and vegetables too.

As I entered the front door of our home, I found Michaela cleaning the kitchen.

"Are you back? What beautiful flowers! Did you get them at the market?"

She moved toward the cabinet to get a vase. "Let me get

some water for those," she said.

"Yes, they're from the market," I replied, "but don't put them in water. I bought them and I want to do it," I explained, looking for a suitable vase.

"Of course," she said and continued to work.

"This one will be great," I said aloud, finding the perfect glass vase. I poured some water into it and added a little sugar, then arranged the irises. I placed the vase on the table in the living room and it lit up the whole area.

"Amazing," I smiled. "Michaela, I'm going upstairs to relax for a bit. If I don't come down later, you can leave, see you tomorrow, okay?"

"Alright," she said, seeming to be more at ease with me now than she was before. "Mrs. Margot?"

"Yes?"

"Should I wash the fruit and vegetables?"

"No, I'll do it later. See you tomorrow," I said and went upstairs to the bedroom.

I took a shower and slipped into something a little more comfortable, then started organizing the clothes in the cupboard again until it was completely reorganized.When I went downstairs Michaela was already gone. Maybe she had announced that she was leaving, but I hadn't heard her.

I washed the fruit and vegetables and made two salads, one fruit salad, and one vegetable salad. I ate a little of both and then made some hot tea. I sat in the living room, turned on the TV, and the wonderful smell of the irises filled the room. The hot tea warmed me and I watched a relaxing movie. Every moment felt beautiful and every moment was important to me.

"Margot!"

Time had passed so quickly, when I looked up, you were home.

"I'm here!"

You came into the living room and saw me. I could tell by

the look on your face you were surprised.

"Hello," you said.

"Hello, how are you? How was your day at work? Do you feel better?"

"Yes, yes," you said. "Who made the salads?"

"I did. I went to the market and bought some fresh fruit and vegetables. Have some," I replied.

"You went to the market?"

"Yes. That's where I picked up these beautiful blue irises. Aren't they gorgeous?"

"Yes, they are," you replied, a little bit unsure of my mood.

"Come sit with me, let's watch this movie together, it's really interesting," I said.

"Not right now."

"Why?"

"I'm tired, another time," you said and went upstairs to the bedroom.

"Okay, night. I'll be here watching the movie," I said.

"Margot?"

You stopped when you were almost halfway up the stairs.

"Yes?"

"The irises smell really nice."

"I know, that's why I love them."

"Now I remember how much you love blue irises."

"Yes, I do love them. I love flowers."

"When we met, that was one of the first things you told me about yourself. You also told me that your father loved flowers, that's why you loved them so much. I didn't buy you irises but I bought you a rose. You probably can't go wrong with a rose," you said, looking at me.

"Probably not," I said.

When we moved here you told me that you wanted to plant blue irises in the garden. The gardener could have done it but you insisted that you wanted to plant them yourself. So that's why most of the garden is still empty, you wanted to fill it all with blue irises, but it never happened," you said in a sad voice.

"It's never too late, Arthur, even when it 's late," I said.

"Do you believe that, Margot?"

"I desperately want to."

You went into the bedroom and I watched the movie, drank my tea, and enjoyed the beautiful blue irises.

Yours,

Margot

P.S. Someone will say that if it was that simple to be happy, everyone would be happy. I agree. Learning to be happy is not simple at all because you'll have to give up the complicated, the complex, and the obscure. You'll have to give up all the labyrinths that lead nowhere and realize that happiness lies in waking up one morning, walking through your neighborhood, going to the market, and buying blue irises, so that your whole house will smell of them.

CHAPTER TEN

August 15, 2019

My dear Arthur,

This morning I woke up earlier than I usually do, but I felt completely rested and refreshed. I was in a great mood. You were still asleep, I couldn't believe it. I was so excited to start my day.

I got up from the sofa and went into the kitchen to make some coffee. It's been a long time since I made myself a good cup of coffee. I used to enjoy that ritual. I made coffee for you too, and remembered that you love strong, pure espresso. The whole house smelled of coffeebeans and the aroma awakened some beautiful memories in me.

"Margot?" I heard you call out from upstairs, and sensed a hint of disbelief in your voice.

"I'm downstairs!" I shouted. "Come down here, I have something for you," I said.

I heard your footsteps on the stairs and in less than a minute you were in the kitchen. You found me sitting at the kitchen counter, drinking my coffee and reading a newspaper. I could tell you were surprised.

"Margot, what is this now?"

"What do you mean? I'm drinking coffee. I made some for you too." I pointed at your cup with my eyes. "Come on." I smiled at you.

"For me?"

"Yes, for you," I replied and continued reading.

"Margot, I have to ask you something," you said, picking up

your coffee and taking a sip.

"Yes?" I lowered the newspaper so that I could see you.

"Margot, have you started taking medication?"

"Why do you ask me that?"

"Well, you're acting differently. It's like you're someone else," you said.

"Arthur, don't worry," I put my hand on top of yours, "everything is fine, I'm not taking any medication," I smiled and drank the last sip of my coffee, then I got up.

"I'm going to take a shower. I want to go out a bit today. See you later, okay?"

I climbed the stairs and from behind I could feel your gaze fixed on me.

In the bedroom I leaned against the door for a moment and repeated what you had asked me in the kitchen; '*Am I taking medication?*' I whispered it softly to myself and for a moment the anxiety almost grabbed me again. I felt I was on the verge of slipping back into those negative thoughts, but I pulled myself back and stopped it.

"I will not allow it," I said to myself.

I understood then that it was not your fault. It's not your fault at all that you think your wife is different when she's happy, and that something's happening to her as soon as she's in a good mood and makes you a cup of coffee. Obviously, I fit the victim mould well, which is probably why I stayed in that mould for so long, but that's changed. I have the instinct now to wrap myself in new colors, which may not fit me perfectly yet, but I'm learning to find reasons to feel joy. I'm not obsessing over a barrage of unanswered questions anymore, I know there is nothing good for me there.

As I am writing this, I recall what my mother said to my late grandmother when my grandmother lost her hair and began wearing a wig. My grandmother, who was sensitive about it, asked my mother,'My daughter, do you think other people will get used to me like this?' My mother smiled and said,'It will

54

happen when you get used to it first'.

I went to take a shower and this time I didn't linger, I got ready very quickly because I was keen to go out. When I got out of the shower, you were in the bedroom picking out a tie.

"I can't decide which one," you said.

"The blue one," I suggested, and you gave me a funny look. I wasn't sure what it meant. I remembered when we first started dating I teased you about dressing up too much, and I thought maybe you were thinking back to that time; or maybe you looked at me funny because I was wrapped in a towel. You hadn't seen me like that in a while.

"Gray, I think gray is a better choice," you said, disagreeing with me.

"Okay," I said, and smiled at you. As I crossed the room to pick out my own outfit, I could feel your eyes on me, watching me. Maybe you thought I'd be upset because you disregarded my suggestion. You consistently never chose what I suggested anyway. Did you expect me to get angry again and start a fight; tell you that you're deliberately hurting my feelings and that you're torturing me? I wasn't about to do that because I'm no longer the woman who is always unhappy when her husband doesn't meet her expectations. You're your own man Arthur, and I'm my own person too. You have your reasons for your behavior, and I have my own. If I spend my time analyzing you and your actions, what's left for me?

"I thought you decided on the gray one?" I said, seeing that you were still undecided.

"Yes, yes, I'm just not sure this looks good together. I don't think I have the perfect tie for this shirt Margot," you said.

"Arthur, you can't live life afraid of not being perfect. You know that," I said, and kissed you on the cheek, not even sure where that inclination came from.

"I'm going. Have a nice day!"

"Thank you," you said, barely audible, and when I reached

the door you called me back and I turned to face you.

"Where are you going today, all dressed up?"

"I'm going for a walk and then I thought I'd go by Les Restos du Cœur, just to see about something."

"You mean that charity that gives food to the needy?"

"Yes."

"What are you going to do there?"

"I want to volunteer," I smiled. "I have to go now Arthur, see you later."

I decided to take the subway instead of my car, and walked to the metro station. I thought it'd be good for me because I hadn't been around people for a long time. I know the weather gets better during the second half of August and people generally walk more this time of year. Everyone was on their way somewhere, some people were in a hurry, some people were trudging along slowly, I simply enjoyed being out in the fresh air. I really felt comfortable in my own skin. I haven't felt like that in ages. It didn't even matter to me if it was hot or cold outside, if it was windy or calm, I was just glad to be out. I felt an overwhelming sense of peace and quiet that came over me through my entire body.

I have to confess this to you, Arthur - I overestimated you and I underestimated myself. You don't have enough power to make me as unhappy as I was. All of that power was always mine. I made myself so unhappy, I had the power. I could have completely destroyed myself. The good news is I can change and I can begin to use my power differently. Maybe one day I'll be able to use my energy to make myself happy instead of sad, and when that happens I can be anything or anyone I choose. I just must decide that's all. I know it's been a long-time coming Arthur, but I think I'm finally on the right track.

I found taking the subway to be a little bit complicated at first, but then I used the Paris Metro app and quickly managed to find my route. It said I had to change railway lines twice and then I had to walk the rest of the way to get to my destination on Clichy Street.

I sat in the first seat on the train, right next to the entrance. It wasn't very crowded. There was an older woman sitting next to me, reading the paper. A young man and a young woman were sitting across from us and they couldn't keep their hands off each other, kissing and embracing like they didn't care who saw. There was another elderly woman sitting next to them, staring at them. I wondered if she felt nostalgic, perhaps remembering her own young love. I looked around and observed the different people surrounding me, realizing how closed off from the world I had been, stuck in my own mind, uninterested in anything, and only obsessed with my own unhappiness. The cry of a small baby got my attention and I turned to look. There was a beautiful, young mother holding her crying baby in her arms. In the past, when I saw a mother with a child I would be suffocated by pain because she had what I wanted - a baby. I didn't feel like that now. I looked at the situation differently and thought, that mother also wants many things she probably doesn't have, same as me or anyone else. I didn't want to be a victim of my desires the way I was before. My hopes and dreams will come true someday, I know they will, in one form or another, but I can't sit around and wait for that to happen. I should always be grateful. When dissatisfaction swallows you all the fulfilled desires in the world won't be enough to make you happy because there will always be something else you think is missing. The dissatisfied person focuses on what he doesn't have, not seeing all the blessings right in front of him.

"Lovely baby," I said.

"Thank you," the woman replied, "she's got a mind of her own. I can't quiet her when I want to. It's really hard."

"Hang in there," I said, understanding that it was difficult for all of us. I hope one day I'll stop comparing my sorrow with everyone else's, that I'll be wise enough to know that the person who has what you don't have, lacks something else that you possess. It's not a sin to long for something that someone else has, but it is great sin not to appreciate what is already yours.

That's why Arthur, from today on I will value my time. I will value my life, and I will fight to remember to cherish it, no matter what the circumstances may be.

I got off the first train and changed railway lines. The second part of the journey was shorter, as there were only two stops. When I got to my station I turned around in circles trying to figure out which direction I ought to take. I started walking, and the excitement of getting involved with something brand new grew.

I got to the building and a woman with a kind smile greeted me.

"Welcome, how can I help you?"

"Good afternoon, I'm Margot, Margot Ango," I said, "this is my first time here, but I'd like to apply to be a volunteer please," I smiled.

"Wonderful! I'm Adrienne," the woman with the polite voice said, "I'm one of the organizers here," she said, holding out her hand, which I took. "Can you fill in this form, we need some personal information."

She handed me a questionnaire and I took out a pen.

"Margot, are you familiar with what we do here at Les Restos du Cœur, and what our goals are?"

"I know a little, but I'm not completely familiar with everything," I smiled. "I just know I want to help," I added as I handed back the forms.

"Great, that's the most important thing, attitude, and the rest can be learned," she said. "We are a charity, and all the projects we implement are intended to address a pressing need in society, and of course, to help someone. You see, we really do a lot of different things here, so you need to think about where you want to place yourself, that way you can serve both our interests best. We always need volunteers, especially those who will work really hard," she explained.

"I want to try," I said, feeling nervous.

"That's good, don't worry, that's very good," she smiled. "We have a lot of volunteers who help us achieve our aims. Some help with preparing food, some prefer working with babies and children, it all depends where you fit best, you see."

"Babies?" I thought that sounded perfect for me.

"Yes, we run a project for young parents and future parents who are facing difficulties. We have a helpdesk and provide material assistance as well as clothes, nappies, baby food, toys, equipment, counseling, paediatric examinations, advice, and whatever else we can. We focus our efforts on babies from birth to the age of twelve months. It's a great help for the parents."

"I understand," my eyes immediately lit up and she saw it.

"Would you like to get involved in this area?"

"I would love to," I replied enthusiastically.

"Do you have any children?" she asked, unaware of how sensitive the question was. My first instinct was to lower my head and be quiet, but I didn't do that.

"I don't have any yet," I said, "but I would very much like to have kids, some day," I smiled.

"I'm sure you will then," we understood each other with one look. "Okay, then it's decided. Now, I suggest we take a walk around, and you can have a look at the departments where these processes take place, and then you can get some idea of how we do things around here."

I smiled and followed her. As we walked through the building, she explained a bit about each room we walked by. We passed many people and Adrienne exchanged a few words with lots of them.

"This is it," she said all of a sudden, pointing to a huge room. One part of the room was full of baby products, neatly arranged, while the other part of the room was a large, empty space, packed with tables and toys.

"Mrs. Adrienne?"

"Can we agree on something? We are a big family here. Can we drop the 'Mrs.' and be on a first name basis? I'm Adrienne, and you're Margot, okay?"

We smiled at each other.

"Alright," I said, embarrassed. "I mean Adrienne, where are the babies examined, that is, where are the paediatric examinations done?"

"You notice everything, don't you? Bravo." She pointed in the direction of an office and said, "Over there, that room. Do you want to see it?"

"I want to, of course," I followed her and we entered the office. It was well equipped and quite large.

"This is Danielle, our paediatrician, or at least, one of our paediatricians. We have two more but they'll only be here in September."

Danielle got up, walked over to me and introduced herself. "Volunteer?"

"I hope so," I sighed.

"Hope is the foundation, and it is often underestimated," Adrienne said, sitting down in a chair. "I've seen many wise men who had no hope - and you can't go anywhere without hope. It's the umbrella that covers you when there's a storm. If you don'thave it, you have nothing," she said, as I listened to her speak."Margot, never let go of hope," she continued, "it is the ground on which you stand, without it there is only a hole," she smiled and began to write something down.

She reminded me a bit of my mother, her words did, and I couldn't hide how much I admired her already, even though we had just met.

Adrienne continued to explain how the charity worked and told me about the different projects they ran there, then left me with Danielle to settle in.

"We call this large space an interactive space, almost everything happens here, and in that part over there we store all the clothes, nappies, food, equipment, toys, and everything you can imagine," Danielle said.

I looked around at the vast space.

Adrienne said I should come back the next day at around ten o'clock the morning so I could slowly start getting involved in projects.She said she would ask one of the more experienced volunteers to guide me through the processes, and said she was sure I'd be great.

"We believe in one thing here," she said, "where there is a desire, everything is possible."

Adrienne took me by the hand and hugged me goodbye."See you tomorrow Margot, okay? Will you be able to find your way out of the building?"

"Yes, thanks Adrienne," I replied, and then remembered I had forgotten to ask her an important question.

"Adrienne, before I forget," I said, and she turned and came toward me.

"Yes, Margot?"

"I want to bring a few things, I want to donate something."

"Of course, that would be wonderful. When you start tomorrow, you'll get a good idea of what we need - so don't rush, everything in time," she said. "See you tomorrow!"

Outside the building I stopped to catch my breath. I thought about the amount of time I had thrown away being unhappy, through my own fault. I'd been chasing dreams that I thought I was entitled to and lost what was right in front of me. We only have the present, I thought, and yet I had persistently squandered my time to serve the void I wanted to fill. On my way home, countless feelings awoke in me. I was changing, and I believed now that I had something to look forward to the next day.

When I got home, Michaela greeted me. She was just getting ready to leave.

"Mrs. Margot, how was your day? You left so early this morning. I didn't even see you," she looked at me with surprise.

"It was great Michaela, really great," I said. "It's still August, so it was nice and warm outside. I'm going upstairs for a bit, I want to organize a few things and take a shower," I added.

"That's right, it is. Okay, see you tomorrow, Mrs. Margot."

"Michaela?" I turned to face her.

"Yes?"

"Drop the 'Mrs.' please, can you? I know you do it out of respect, but we already know each other and we see each other every day. I know that you respect me and I want you to know that I respect you too, but from now on I'm just Margot to you, okay?" I smiled, and Michaela smiled back, leaving me wondering why I hadn't told her that before.

"Alright, Margot," she said, taking her bag. "See you tomorrow," she opened the front door and left.

I took a shower and the water cooled my whole body. Afterward, I sat down at my laptop and started doing research on the internet. I wanted to know more about the different kinds of help that babies and mothers needed, where there were gaps in the system that had to be filled. I read some articles and watched YouTube videos, I was hungry for new information and for ideas.

You were tired when you got home. I was still working on the computer when you came into the bedroom.

"What are you doing?"

"Just something," I said, sweetly.

"How did it go today?"

I looked up and saw you were taking off your shirt.

"It went well, I'm going in again tomorrow."

"So you're serious about this?"

"Dead serious."

"That's great," you paused and then continued, "we'll see how long this euphoria lasts."

"I think it will last. I'll go to the living room if you want to sleep. I want to watch some videos before I go to bed."

"Yes, I'm very tired," you said.

"Alright, then, good night."

I picked up the laptop and left the room, sat in the living room for hours, unable to stop researching. It was really nice. The day had left me inspired, and then I started writing this letter to you. Writing letters helps me. I don't know how and why this happens, but I know that it helps me, and at the moment - that's all I need.

Yours,
Margot

P.S. When you asked me how long this euphoria would last, I wanted to answer, 'While I have hope.'

You and I still have something, Arthur, but it's broken and maybe it's not enough - but it's still there. So perhaps we too, have hope.

CHAPTER ELEVEN

August 16, 2019

My dear Arthur,

I was hurting so much and for the longest time I couldn't find the real cause of my suffering. What was the point of all my pain? It took a while before I could look at it from a different perspective. I'm finding new answers to all my questions - perhaps this will make the hurt meaningful. It's hard to fight Arthur, but if you decide not to give up, every day gets easier.

Yesterday while I was researching on the internet, an idea came to me that I couldn't wait to share with Adrienne at Les Restos du Cœur. When I woke up the bedroom door upstairs was closed, and I assumed you were still asleep. I made coffee for both of us and toasted some bread with jam and butter. It used to be our favorite breakfast, just eating it together made us happy – but we stopped doing that completely. After I made breakfast, you appeared on the stairs and said, "Margot, you're busy again," and you came down and sat at the counter.

"Good morning Arthur, how are you?" I looked at you.

"I'm good. Just surprised to see you like this," you said, looking at the breakfast. "Bread, with jam and butter. Our favorite," you said.

"Yes, it used to be one of our morning rituals. Rituals are really important, we shouldn't let them just fall away, don't you agree?" I handed you the coffee and the plate.

"It hasn't fallen away. I still eat bread with jam and butter for breakfast every day," you said and took a sip of your coffee.

"Oh?" I sipped my coffee as well.

"Yes, I just have breakfast at work, alone, that's all."

"I see."

"I eat quickly, before my meetings start."

"I knew you had to be eating somewhere but I wasn't sure where. I thought maybe it was somewhere better than here with me."

I don't know why I said that. There was silence. Your expression changed and then you said, "Margot, I want you to know something, even when we were at our most challenging times, I didn't think it could be better somewhere else. That would be like admitting defeat, and I don't accept defeat. I'm a winner. I don't give up on what I want. I'm just sorry that my power as a husband is limited," you sighed, and took a bite of your breakfast.

"Is your power limited?"

"It's limited because the woman who decides to be unhappy will be unhappy. I can't do anything about that, no matter how much I love you," you looked at me with your deep brown eyes, and it seemed as if there was pain there, pain which you were unable to hide this time.

There was silence again. Neither of us knew what else to say.

"Margot, thank you for the coffee and breakfast," you said, getting up.

"Arthur, there's more," I said.

"I'm full. Are you going out Margot?"

"Yes."

You turned around before leaving and said, "Just because I'm full doesn't mean I'm not happy that there's more left," you smiled.

"Of course. There will be other days, Arthur," I smiled too.

"It's a nice day out, where are you going?"

"To Les Restos du Cœur again. I have some new ideas."

"That's great. I hope it turns out the way you want."

"Thanks, have a nice day," I said, and our eyes met, saying

many things we could not say out loud. There are other days, I thought. Maybe on those days the time will be right. I stayed in the kitchen to drink my coffee.

You got ready for work and left while I waited for Michaela to arrive. In the silence of my loneliness, I thought about our brief conversation, the pain in your eyes, and the sincerity. I felt like I was in unknown and undiscovered territory, and it was changing my monotonous world - which for so long, I had mistakenly thought was the only truth there was for me. I forgot that truth changes, it grows, and matures. I locked my truth away behind four walls and turned it sour. Things and people change, and things that were once big and relevant can become small and almost invisible. Isn't that sad, Arthur? Isn't it tragic to let your truth turn into a world that simply makes no sense?

"Mrs. Margot?" I heard Michaela's voice say, "sorry, I mean, Margot, I think I'll need a minute to get used to not having to be formal with you," she said with a grin as she entered the house.

"You'll get used to it, change is beautiful," I said, "I'm going upstairs, I need to get ready."

"See you later," said Michaela, when I greeted her before leaving, and I could feel the joy in her voice as she said goodbye to me and sent me off with a happy face.

I took the subway again, but this time I wanted to walk a little further than I had before. I knew I had enough time before my appointment at ten o'clock.

The train was very full. I stood beside the entrance, surrounded by many different people. There was a grandmother and grandfather on my left-hand side, sitting next to each other, arguing. Opposite me, there were two boys looking at their phone screens and laughing out loud. Higher up from them, there was a lady who stood holding a puppy in her arms. The puppy was restless, like he wanted to jump onto one of the boys' laps. I couldn't stop myself from laughing and the lady glared at me.

When the train started to slow down the lady with the puppy headed for the door I was standing next to, and as she passed me she said, "Everyone has their own problems, honey. It's not easy for any of us, not even for him," she pointed at her puppy, kissed him, and stepped off the train.

I got off soon after her and walked through the streets of Paris. I had the urge to get to know this city better. Paris is one of the most beautiful cities in the world. There are so many interesting places, museums, and parks to visit. The city is bustling with stories. I thought of all the love songs written under the Parisian sky. At one time I hated Paris so much because it felt so empty to me. I called it Paris, the city of darkness. I never thought that maybe the darkness came from inside.

The walk did me good. I arrived at Les Restos du Cœur faster than I expected, and was greeted by Adrienne.

"Margot, you're here."

"Yes, I'm on time, right?" I looked at her worriedly.

"Yes, yes, don't worry. I have to go out, but Danielle is waiting for you. Will you manage on your own?" She paused, looked at me, and smiled, then said, "You will manage," and she left. "I'll see you later," she shouted.

I felt a bit lost, but was determined to be independent. I walked slowly and shyly, looking at people I passed, my legs felt like jelly but I kept moving forward. Shortly, I came to the right door and saw Danielle.

"Margot, there you are. Come on in. We have a lot of work to do," she said, extending her hand to me. Her handshake was firm.

"How are you, Danielle?" I asked.

"I'm fine, a few new people came in this morning, all at once, but we managed," she sighed. "Come on, we'll start here," she showed me the section of the room that was full of baby products.

"So many," I said.

"Yes, they brought a lot of products this morning and they're not packed in proper order, but you and I will change that. I'll help you, but if a mother comes in for an examination I'll have to leave you to attend to her, is that okay?" She spoke very gently.

"Of course," I said.

"Margot, there is no perfect method to do this, we just need to sort everything out, one by one. Let's arrange all the same type of products in the same order - that ought to give it some structure. Are you in?"

"Great. I like it when everything is in order. It's a pity that you can't organize everything in life like that," I said as I started sorting out the products.

"Oh, that'san endless struggle that goes on for as long as we're alive," Danielle said.

"What do you mean?"

"I mean discovering, learning, growing, the journey - it's an endless process, it never stops. There is never a final answer or a final destination," she explained. Her words made me feel sad.

"So there's no peace you mean?" I stopped for a while and looked at her. She raised her head and seemed surprised.

"Are you looking for peace, Margot?"

"Well, yes," I said, unsure of myself.

"Peace is in the journey. Peace is in the quest. Peace is in the uncertainty. Peace is in the temptation. Peace is in the routine of the day. Peace is in you," she touched my shoulder, "if you don't find it in yourself, you won't find it anywhere."

I didn't say anything, I kept working until a mother with a baby came in for an examination. Danielle excused herself and said she would be back shortly. I packed all the products perfectly, still thinking of what Danielle had said. Her words intrigued me. I wanted to know what she meant, but I also wasn't sure I wanted to know. What she said made me feel gloomy, but she looked like a woman who really understood life. I thought she was wise, and I wondered how she knew so much, but I didn't dare to ask.

Time passed without my noticing, and I did my job well.

"Margot, you're like a machine," I heard Danielle's voice behind me.

"Is this okay?" I asked excitedly.

"It's great! I don't think this section has ever been sorted out so neatly," she smiled.

"Not true," I laughed.

"You're a Virgo, aren't you?"

"Yes, in fact it's my birthday in nine days. How did you know?"

"I recognize a Virgo when I see one. There is no star sign that knows how to organize things better, but also somehow complicate matters."

She laughed playfully when she said that, and I laughed too.

"We deserve a little rest," she said. "Shall we go for coffee? There's a cafe at the end of the street."

"Sure, why not," I agreed, and we left immediately.

When we got to the cafe, we sat down at the first free table and waited for someone to come over and take our order. While we waited I watched the people around me, and I must have sighed without even knowing it, because Danielle asked me if I was tired.

"No," I replied.

"It's nothing to hide if you are, it's only human. You just have to keep going, that's all." I felt embarrassed and looked down.

"How old are you, Margot?"

"Thirty-two, I'll be thirty-three in nine days," I replied.

"So you're thirty-two now?"

"Yes, but in nine days ..."

"Margot, I didn't ask you how old you will be, I asked how

old you are now," she said, sweetly.

"Yes, I understand," I began to laugh.

"Are you married?"

"Yes," I said, as the waiter arrived at our table.

"Espresso for me please, and for you?"

I nodded.

"Two espressos, please," she said, and the waiter left.

"So you're married. Children?"

I tried not to reveal my emotions.

"No," I shrugged.

"You want children, don't you?"

"Very much," I sighed again, holding back a tear.

"It will happen. I'm sure of it, when the time is right," she said confidently.

"You think so?" I asked her as if she could predict my life.

"Yes, I do. Do you doubt it?"

"We've been trying for a year, but nothing's happened yet. The doctors said that everything is fine - medically, I mean. They told us we just need more time because we haven't been trying for long enough to worry about it. I wanted it to happen right away and I wanted it so much. The waiting was killing me. It stopped my life dead in its tracks. Our daily lives seemed to sink like a ship," I said.

It was so easy to speak to Danielle. There was something comforting about speaking to a stranger who wouldn't judge me.

The waiter brought our coffees and I took a sip of my bitter espresso.

"We just feel so disconnected from each other," I said. My husband works all the time and denies it's an avoidance tactic. He said he must focus on his career to give us a good life. He has an important job, I understand that, he works at SFR the telecommunication company - he's part of the First Team. I knew that his work was important to him when we first met, but

I never realized how hard it would be on me to be alone all the time. He just always has somewhere else to be while I'm stuck alone at home. We eventually ended up spending less and less time together, and our intimate life seems to have disappeared completely. I realized that I was no longer living with my husband, but merely sharing a house with a stranger," I said, taking a sip of my coffee and bearing my soul to Danielle.

Danielle listened to me and said, "Margot, I don't think anything in life is accidental, not even our meeting today. I'm thirty-four years old. I know I look younger, but there are reasons why I don't look my age. Four years ago I had a very difficult miscarriage. The doctors saved me but I came very close to losing my life. They told me that the consequences were irreversible and that my chances of having a child now are about one percent. I thought the life I always wanted was over for me. I love children and wanted kids of my own very much. It was hard but I had to come to terms with my fate. I didn't want to worsen the trauma I already felt. My partner couldn't deal with it. We broke up and I was all alone. It was the worst thing that ever happened to me, but it was also the best thing. Thanks to all the pain, I managed to overcome my biggest fear. I had missed out on incredible opportunities in life by being sad and mourning what I didn't have. I've learned that the magic of life is looking around you and noticing what's beautiful. Don't ache for answers - just be completely comfortable in your skin. I finally feel comfortable in my skin and I love my life now. That's why life loves me back. Love works like that, it comes back to you," she said, putting her hand on mine gently.

As I listened to her story my problems started to feel incredibly small.

"There will always be questions we can't answer and there will always be people asking those questions. Don't be that way toward yourself or toward anyone else. It's a path that will never bring you happiness," she said.

I couldn't help it; I couldn't hide my tears and they began to stream down my face.

"Danielle, my marriage is ruined and I don't even know

how or when it happened," I said, trembling.

She reached out and held my hand.

"I want to tell you something," she said, "you should never let your life stop. Patience is a wonderful trait, but waiting is something else entirely. If you're waiting with folded arms, almost frozen, and doing nothing else, then you're not being patient. Patient people go on with their lives, they live every day, and though they always carry inner desires which they hope will be fulfilled, it doesn't mean they base their whole life on those desires. You see Margot, patience is not waiting, patience is moving forward. Patience doesn't mean you're not happy here and now," she smiled at me, and my tears continued to flow from my eyes.

"That's exactly what I was thinking," I wiped my moist cheeks. "Please, do you want to talk about something else?"I wanted to change the subject and smiled shyly.

"Of course," she said softly.

"Danielle, yesterday I was watching some videos and projects online. I've been researching, so that I can figure out how to contribute to this organization. I don't want to sound like I think I'm some genius who came up with some amazing idea, but I have a suggestion. In Barcelona there's this human rights group called the Barcelona Women's Network, which supports and advocates for the rights of women and children. I thought we could collaborate with them - maybe have a workshop educating them on what we do here for babies, so that they can do it there too - like advocacy. What do you think?" I looked at her uncertainly. As I spoke, she had a gentle smile on her face the whole time.

"That sounds great! I like it! I think I know that organization. Of course, we'll have to talk to Adrienne to see what she thinks, and then we should contact the Barcelona Women's Network as well."

"Of course," I smiled. "Danielle, you made my day better, thank you, thank you for everything," I said. "Your courage inspires me," I added, and she continued to warm me with her smile.

After we finished our coffee and our conversation we agreed to meet the next day at the organization's office and talk about my idea. Going back home, I was on a high and it felt as if I had released a part of myself to freedom. A sense of relief came over me. I felt that someone had touched me directly in the wound that hurt the most, and at the same time it started to heal.

By the time I got home Michaela had already left. I realized I had eaten almost nothing during the day. I made a big salad, ate a portion, and left the rest for you Arthur. I went up to our bedroom and took a shower. Cold water dripped over my body and all my emotions were raw. I felt different, more alive than I could remember ever being.

Coming out of the bathroom I heard your voice. I looked at the clock in the bedroom and noticed it was earlier than the usual time you came home.

"Margot?"

"I'm coming," I replied, looping my bathrobe around my waist, and I went downstairs. When you saw me, you seemed pleased.

"What are you doing?"

"I took a shower," I said, "and I made us a salad. Would you like some?"

"No, not now," you said, looking at me.

"How was your day? Mine was great."

"Good - boring. Meetings - problems. The usual," you said, slowly coming toward me.

I felt self-conscious and took a step back. You stopped and sighed.

"I'll go upstairs and get ready," I said, "and then I think I'll do more research."

"Okay," you said, "I'll watch TV downstairs, and maybe I'll try some of that salad."

Upstairs, I closed the bedroom door and sat down on the bed. I was scared because I didn't know if you wanted to try to touch me or if you wanted to kiss me, but the unexpected attempt at intimacy was too much, too soon for me. I may have hurt you by withdrawing, but I really didn't know what else to do. Today when I cried with Danielle, I realized all my feelings are still there.

As I'm writing this letter, you are downstairs. I don't know if you're asleep or awake, but I feel that you're as confused as I am. I don't know how to behave around you. Writing these letters became a way for me to discover my hidden world. I think everyone should talk to themselves at the end of their day Arthur. It's a good way to see where you went wrong. It can make you realize that when you thought you were at your wisest, you were in fact at your most irrational.

Yours,

Margot

P.S. Do you think it's possible to lose someone and then find them again at a different time? Do you think that maybe people split from each other so that they can be more right for each other when they meet the next time? Do you think this could happen? I'm starting to think it can.

CHAPTER TWELVE

August 17, 2019

My dear Arthur,

This morning I woke up early again, it has become a wonderful new habit to do this.When I opened my eyes I thought, life rarely goes according to the plans we make, but that doesn't mean we shouldn't plan - we should plan but we shouldn't expect. If something happens that's different to what we planned, we shouldn't despair. Planning is a platform which helps us to organize our time, but that platform is not our life. I want to really start practicing this belief, to plan so that it makes my life easier instead of more difficult. What I mean is, I set some goals in the past, and while I was waiting for them to be realized, I allowed sadness to flourish because I had to wait. I never grasped that the waiting period is called life. I never thought of it this way. I never thought that I hold all the cards in my hands and that what I dislike, I can change. We humans are funny. We are eternal wanderers in search of happiness, yet happiness can be found so easily, hidden in the little things, completely accessible to the person who knows how to understand its essence.

I went downstairs and made coffee for the two of us. I thought it would be great if it could become our shared ritual again. You woke up half an hour after me, and immediately started looking for me.

"Margot, are you downstairs?"

"Yes, Arthur, I'm downstairs," I shouted. "There's coffee," I added, and you immediately came to the kitchen.

"I'm so into coffee right now," you said, "I'll get dressed for work after I finish this cup," you smiled like a small child, your hair tousled from sleeping. At that moment it was clear that we're uncomfortable around each other, even though we know each other. We're like two strangers meeting, nervous, with a sense of uncertainty, but at the same time, there is the promise of something more.

"Margot," you said, sipping your coffee. "This coffee is nice."

"Thank you," I said.

"Margot, I wanted to ask you something," your voice trembled. "It's your birthday in a few days. I wanted to suggest we go to the villa in Antibes, to spend some time there. Today is Saturday, your birthday is next week so we can leave for Antibes on Thursday, stay for a few days, and celebrate your birthday there. We can get back on Sunday night. What do you think?"

You looked at me then looked away, as if you were afraid of my answer.

I was silent, I didn't know what to say. I felt a rebirth of energy between us. It seemed to be a miracle, but I wasn't sure if I was the only one who felt it. What scared me was the idea that our reconnection would bring us back to the same problems, awakening in me the version of myself that I never wanted to see again. I was finally aware that I was responsible for my own life and my own happiness, but I still wasn't sure I was strong enough.

"Margot, what do you think?"

I knew I had to say something."Alright, let's go. I love Antibes," I smiled, not knowing exactly what I was getting into.

"Antibes loves you too. The whole world loves you, you just have to give it a chance," you said and drank your coffee, then got up from your chair."I have to go, thanks for the coffee. What are you doing today?"

"I'm going to Les Restos du Cœur again to drop off some nappies and help out. Yesterday I came up with an idea I want to pitch to them, so today we're going to talk about it," I explained.

"Even on a Saturday? Bravo. You surprise me."

"I'm surprising myself too," I whispered, drinking my coffee and feeling good that every new day I continued building from where I left off.

After you left Michaela came and I exchanged a few words with her, then I went upstairs to get ready. "You look beautiful Margot," Michaela said when I came back downstairs, dressed.

"Thank you," I said.

"Are you going out again," she asked.

"Yes, I'm going out. I've actually started going to this place called Les Restos du Cœur. It's a charity," I said.

"Yes, yes, I know it, I know it very well."

"I'm volunteering there. They have a department which works with babies. It helps parents and future parents who are financially struggling, by donating clothes, nappies, material support, offering paediatric examinations, giving advice, and so much more. I have some ideas that might contribute to the growth of the project, so we'll see what happens…I wanted to volunteer in this department. I liked the idea of helping with babies," I said, and my eyes said everything I could not.

"How beautiful to see you falling in love with life," Michaela said, suddenly hugging me.

"Michaela, thank you," I sighed. "Thank you for everything!"

"Margot, I did nothing," she said.

"Yes, you did, you did more than you think," I said and hugged her even tighter.

"I have to go," I pulled loose and walked to the door. "Have a nice day!" I shouted, then I turned to give her one big smile.

"Have a nice day, Margot," she said, giving me a look filled with joy and pride.

Getting out of the house felt good and I was determined to make as many donations to Les Restos du Cœur as possible, so

I got into my car and set off, planning to fill the whole backseat with nappies. I stopped at Monopri, not far from home, and bought as many packs of nappies as I could. I left feeling good. There were not very many people there so I managed to do it quickly. I began to believe that when you want to do something good, the whole universe stands by you and helps you as much as it can. I loaded the packs into the car and headed for Les Restos du Cœur.

As I was driving, I became aware of the silence in my car. I've always loved music, but whenever we've traveled togetherArthur, I'd tell you the music in the car was too loud. I don't know why it was difficult for me to enjoy the things that I loved, or where I picked up the constant need to find reasons to be upset. I decided to put some music on now, and I looked in the compartment at the bottom of the car door to see if I still had some of the old compact discs I used to keep there. In the past I took them everywhere with me. I found them, and threw them on the passenger seat. Among the cd's, I spotted Edith Piaf's cover. 'I haven't heard her angelic voice for a long time,' I thought. I didn't know if I'd be able to stand it when I heard her voice again, but deep down I knew you couldn't die from what once made you feel so alive. Longing for all the feelings you felt and not knowing if you would be able to feel them ever again, can only hurt.

I remember when I met you Arthur, one of our first conversations was about music. When you told me that your favorite singer is Edith Piaf, I knew you'd be able to understand my soul - because her music has always been a cure for me. When I moved to Paris and became your wife I brought my favorite album, *I Do Not Regret Anything* by Edith Piaf, along. I had bought it in 2014 and kept it as one of my most precious possessions. I remember when we moved into our house in Paris, we spent the first night eating pizza on the floor because our furniture had not been bought yet.

"This is a new beginning for us, that's why I wanted to move into a new home," you said.

"I know, but I still brought something old, something

wonderful," I said, and I took Edith Piaf's album out of my bag and played it on the old music system, the one I didn't part with while I was living in Roubaix. Edith's voice echoed through the house, and my favorite song, "Love Is" became the first song we heard between the walls of our new home. I closed my eyes and danced, and you came to me and hugged me. We squeezed into each other like that, dancing slowly. The music was enough and we didn't need anything else. At that moment I was sure I was madly in love with you. Back then, I couldn't know that after we filled our house with beautiful furniture, that happiness would be lost somewhere, that the music would stop, and love would be swallowed up by the silence that felt more alive than the people in that house. I couldn't have known that the house of music would slowly turn into a home of silence and sorrow.

As I drove, my hands trembled, but I managed to open the album and put one of the two CD's in the car's music system. I played the song "I Do Not Regret Anything" and when I heard Edith's voice, tears filled my eyes. These were not sad tears, but tears that appear only when it's time for a change. The whole picture began to make sense. Me, Edith's voice, the car, and the road ahead -I got goosebumps all over my skin, but it wasn't out of pain. It became clear to me that just as it is sung in the song, I too, regret absolutely nothing. I'm ready for a change and although life will never be the same again, it doesn't mean itwon't be beautiful.

I reached the office of Les Restos du Cœur and quickly found a parking spot. I took out some nappy bags, headed for the entrance, and greeted Danielle, who was talking on her phone. She smiled as soon as she saw me and raised her hand,giving me the signal to wait while she wrapped up her conversation.

She interrupted her chat to ask me, "Margot, what is this?"

"Nappies," I said.

"These are a lot of nappies," she smiled and said goodbye to the person she was on the phone with.

"Yes, but I noticed that you needed them."

"That's right," I felt her beautiful energy, which always left me feeling encouraged.

"Let me help you get these inside," she said.

"I can do it, I have some more in the car."

"More?"

"Yes."

"Then I'll take these and you can go get the rest. We'll meet inside, okay?"

"Okay," I said, and slowly handed her all the bags.

Returning to the car, I picked up the rest of the nappies and headed back into the building. I felt useful being at Les Restos du Cœur. I promised myself that I would never let this wonderful feeling leave me.I went in and slowly headed for the room that we worked from. Danielle was already packing the nappies.

"Here I am," I shouted.

"Margot," she said, approaching me and hugging me. She whispered, "A person who wants to help, wants to help themselves too, because by helping others, we are helping ourselves." I put my bags on the floor and quietly let her words sink in.

"Where should I put them; and where should I leave my things?"

"You can put them here and you can leave your things in this locker. We leave all our personal things here."

"Margot, I'll be busy later, I have babies coming for examinations, but we'll see each other soon and talk to Adrienne about your idea, is that alright?"

"Okay, great," I said, feeling very content.

While working, I didn't really think about the things I usually think about. I could see now how important it is for each person to have something of their own, something to fulfill him or her. Looking at all the mothers who came in with their babies, I thought that for us women, that thing often becomes our children. It is in essence very sad, because children grow up and the day comes when they live their own lives. A parent wants to raise children who are independent when they grow up, yet when that happens the woman is empty-handed again, and the need to feel needed doesn't fade.

As I worked, I understood how important the work of Les Restos du Cœur was. It helps young parents and future parents to cope with their responsibilities, and encourages them to have goals outside of being a parent. As I packed, I made a promise to myself Arthur, I don't know if I'll be a mother one day, and I'll try not to think about it anymore, but no matter what happens, I always want to have something of my own. I want to be busy, because the person who has all the time in the world is focused on thinking about what life should be like, and forgets to really live it. I know very well what it means to be such a person, but I never want to do that to myself again.

"Margot, how are you doing?" Danielle said as she came in. "Well done, you finished so much in such a short time!"

"Thanks a lot," I smiled, continuing to work.

"Why don't you take a break and meet me in Adrienne's office, then we can talk," Danielle smiled.

When I got to Adrienne's office, Danielle was already saying something to her about my idea. They were both smiling, which looked like a good sign. I was really excited about the conversation. I couldn't wait to hear what Adrienne thought. I wanted big things for the organization and I really wanted to contribute.

"Margot," Adrienne said, after she asked me to have a seat, "Danielle told me you suggested a collaboration with the Barcelona Women's Network. I know that organization, I've heard about them, and I honestly think they do great work. As for the help we offer here to young and future parents with their babies, so far we haven't reached out to any other organizations to share our skills and expertise. I'd like to hear more about your idea. How do you envisage such a project being structured?"

"Adrienne," I said, "in my mind it would be an educational collaboration between Les Restos du Cœur and the Barcelona Women's Network, implemented to result in a similar output as their current range of services, and offered within their immediate geographical community. I think something like this should be rolled out beyond borders, and with the experience that Les Restos du Cœur has, we can share information and experience with other charitable and social justice groups, focused especially on women, to try and develop the same project in other locations," I said, exhaling a big breath.

"Alright, that is definitely possible. What we could organize are free workshops on our premises, to conduct educational seminars and exchange practical knowledge, and then everything after that would be in their hands. They would have to allocate funds from their budget to provide for travel, accommodation, and further realization of the project. At Les Restos du Cœur, we get our funding from public grants and some private donations. Unfortunately, we're not in a position to offer them resources beyond what I've just said. I don't know what their budget is or what funding they have available."

"I see," I said, concerned that maybe the whole idea was useless, as there was always the possibility that the organization in Barcelona wouldn't have finances to carry out the project either.

"The idea is great, Margot," Adrienne encouraged me. "I really like it."

"The idea is wonderful," Danielle agreed.

"I leave this to you. Get in touch with the right people in Barcelona, talk to them, and see if they're interested. If we find a common language we can organize a workshop here and invite them to come and see how we work, and from there we'll see, what do you think?"

"Great," my eyes lit up.

"I have to go now, but we'll keep in touch on this," Adrienne added, looking at Danielle and I, and then she left the office.

After Adrienne left, I felt a bit unsure if the project was feasible. Danielle sat down next to me.

"What's the matter with you?"

"Nothing, I just realized that the idea would be in vain if the Barcelona Women's Network can't source the finances to realize it."

"Margot, why do you think so far in advance? Why do you do that to your own mind? There are no pointless ideas and there are no pointless changes. We're already changing something, just because we have an idea to change something. Sometimes you just have to let it go. It's useful to plan, but you can't plan for every circumstance, Margot. Focus on the moment, on what we can influence. In other words, contact the organization and start from there," Danielle smiled, and I immediately felt better.

"You possess some kind of a special energy," I said.

"Once you survive, you'll see how much you want to live," she said and stood up.

"Yes," I agreed, getting up as well.

She looked at the paperwork on her desk and said, "I have something else to finish up, are you done?"

"Yes, I'm done."

"Good. Go home, rest. Tomorrow is Sunday. Make a plan and start acting on Monday. Agreed?"

"Alright," I shrugged, "thank you, Danielle."

"You're welcome," she smiled.

I gathered all of my things from the locker and left the building. In my car I played Edith's album again and drove home listening to her voice. I felt that many things were waiting for me. I haven't felt that way in a long time, it was nice, but also incredibly different. When I got home, Michaela was still there and she asked me how my day went.

"Great," I said, "we have a lot of work ahead of us, if my idea works out, that is."

"Wonderful," she said, "Margot, should I prepare something

to eat?"

"No, I'll make a light dinner tonight, you can leave."

"Now?"

"Yes, go ahead. I won't need anything further today."

"It's still early," she said, hesitating.

"Don't worry," I touched her arm. "I'm going upstairs to change and I'll come down later to make some supper. See you tomorrow."

Michaela was still getting used to the new me and gave me a long look, but satisfied that I would make dinner myself, she left.

Later after I rested, I opened the refridgerator trying to decide what to make. I found mascarpone cheese and remembered that we enjoyed a dollop of that on pancakes, with slices of fruit. We had blackberries. Michaela knew we liked it so she always bought a bunch. We had cheese, eggs, milk, and butter as well, but we didn't seem to have flour, vanilla extract, and cinnamon. I scratched through the pantry and after some hunting, I managed to find flour and cinnamon, then after some more hunting, I finally found some vanilla in between the spices. I started making the pancakes and couldn't wait for you to come home when it was ready. I wanted to set it up so that it looked all pretty. I wanted to surprise you at least a little. Toward the end of the preparations, I had not yet set the table, and you came in.

"Margot, is that you?" I heard you shouting my name from the door.

"Of course," I smiled.

"What smells like that?"

I listened to your footsteps and waited impatiently to see how you would react when you saw what I was busy with in the kitchen.

When I saw you, I said, "Pancakes with mascarpone and blackberries, just like in the old days, remember? I'll set the table for us, sit down and relax."

"I haven't eaten pancakes in forever. In fact, I think the last time I ate them was with you, at home," you said, "I'm starving! Can we tuck in? You don't have to move a single thing, I'll come over there," you said, putting your briefcase down and going to the sink to wash your hands.You loosened your tie and sat down on the barstool. "Don't set fancy plates, we'll eat them like this, together."

In that momentI felt as if nothing had changed, as if we had managed to tear down a brick wall and hold each other again.

I sat down on the other chair and we ate, spreading the cheese and arranging the blackberries. It was delicious and incredibly enjoyable.

"These are so good," you said.

"I'm so glad you're enjoying them."

"You dropped one blackberry!"

"Where?"

"On your shirt, don't you see?"

I took a towel, moistened it with a little water and came nearer to you to clean it off.

"I have a stain," you said, as I rubbed it with the wet cloth.

"Don't worry, it'll come out," I said wiping it away. As I cleaned your shirt, I noticed your hand on my face, and you raised my head upwards gently and kissed me. I didn't know how to react so I walked away.

"Margot, I'm sorry. I know it's not like before, but I hoped it could be," you said.

"I'm sorry, I hoped that too," I replied.

"No. I'm the one who's sorry. Thank you for the pancakes, they were delicious. I'm going upstairs."

I watched you slowly climb the stairs to our bedroom, your gaze betraying that I had hurt you.

I stayed in the kitchen for a while doing nothing, just standing still. Everything was unclear. I tidied up the kitchen and sat down in the living room. I picked up a piece of paper and knew it was time to talk to myself. The most honest conversation takes place on a piece of paper. I think I'm getting to know myself again this way.

As I'm writing this, you're upstairs and have been upstairs for some time. I'm imagining you trying to fall asleep, feeling like it's a refuge from what happened between us tonight. Maybe I hurt you by pulling away, but I don't know who is really injured here. I used to think it was me. Now I think maybe it's you too, and if that's the case then we have both been suffering.

Yours,
Margot

P.S. When you kissed me, I kissed you back. As we kissed, I got scared and walked away. The kiss didn't scare me. I was scared by the way we kissed because that's how lovers kiss.

CHAPTER THIRTEEN

August 18, 2019

My dear Arthur,

I really didn't expect this day to be like this. After I made our morning coffee my phone rang, and when I heard my mother's voice I immediately thought something bad happened.

"Margot, it's me. Are you awake? I must have woken you up," she said.

"No Mom, I'm awake. I get up early. Are you okay? Did something happen?"

"No, no. Everything is fine, I'm fine. I'm in Paris, Margot. I came to surprise you for your birthday."

"To surprise me for my birthday?" I was definitely surprised. "My birthday is in seven days," I said.

"I know, but Arthur told me you were going to Antibes on Thursday so I wanted to see you before then."

"Arthur? Did you speak to Arthur?"

"Yes, Margot. He is my daughter's husband and I can speak to him, right? We will talk when we see each other, I've just arrived at Gare du Nord. Will you come and pick me up? To be honest, two hours and thirty minutes is a long journey for an old woman like me," she said, laughing.

After she retired she liked to joke that she was old, even though she is younger in spirit than I am, even when I was a child she was young at heart.

"You're not old, Mom," I smiled, "I'll be there shortly, have a coffee while you wait."

"You're awake," I said, finding you upstairs in the bedroom. "I was just talking to my mother. She's here in Paris and wants me to come pick her up at Gare du Nord. I made coffee if you want some."

You nodded. "I spoke to her on the phone earlier, she said she's coming for your birthday. She wanted to surprise you," you said while knotting your tie.

"Why didn't you tell me?"

"Because she wanted to surprise you," you repeated. "Thanks for the coffee, I could get used to coffee every morning," you said, changing the subject, then added, "if you decide not to do it anymore - I'll miss it."

I got dressed as fast as I could, hurrying to get to my mother. When I went downstairs you had already drank all the coffee, down to the last sip, and left for work.

In the car I was greeted by Edith's beautiful voice. Along the drive, all the way to Gare du Nord, I thought about all the questions my mother usually asked me. At Gare du Nord, I parked and phoned her to let her know I was there.

"I'm here, right in front of the entrance," I said.

"I'm coming," she said out of breath.

"Are you okay?" I worried. My anxiety made me think of the worst.

"Yes, Margot, I'm fine," she said, and then I saw her coming out of the station. She was smiling and she waved at me. She wore her favorite long dress. It had so many colors in it. I always thought it was too bright, but for some reason whenever she wore it, it looked perfect on her. She was walking slower than usual, I immediately noticed that. I had not seen my mother in a long time, and I realized that I had missed her.

I got out of the car to help her with her luggage, even though she was only carrying a small bag and a large paper bag.

"Mom, how are you?"

I hugged her.

"Margot, I love you," she hugged me back tightly.

"I love you too," I said. "Let me help you with your things."

"Put them in the back," she said, and we got in the car and drove off.

"Edith?"

"Yes," I smiled.

"I'm glad you didn't forget the things that make you happy."

"Maybe I forgot, maybe I'm refreshing my memory now."

"Now that's something," she sighed. "Margot, I'm really glad to see you. Arthur told me you were leaving for Antibes on Thursday and I just had to see you for your birthday. I was very worried about you, Margot. I think I felt every drop of your sadness."

I was quiet, hoping that she would stop talking about it, but she didn't.

"Margot, I thought that when you came to Paris things would change. I thought everything would be different with Arthur, but as I can see, you can't escape your pain. Wherever you go, sorrow is with you. I can't understand, despite so many reasons for joy, you persistently choose to be sad. I told you before you left, I told you that now you should forget about everything and start all over again, to allow yourself to be happy. And what did you do? You came to Paris and despite all its beauty, you kept being sad. My Margot," she lowered her head and her voice began to tremble as if she were crying.

I wasn't surprised by her words, but I felt like she was saying more than I could handle. My mother never knew how to pick the right moment to say something, but she tried. Maybe it would be different this time.

"Mom, I'm much better now. We haven't seen each other and we haven't talked, so you don't know, but I've been working on myself. I'm still far from perfect, but I'm progressing every day. I look at things differently now, Mom," I said trying to reassure her.

"Really?"

"Really," I said.

"Arthur said that you're fine. He said that for the first time you've been focused on yourself and that makes him happy."

"Did Arthur say that?"

"Yes, he did."

"I didn't know that Arthur noticed that I was focused on myself."

"Maybe you don't realize what Arthur is like," she said.

At home Michaela was there to welcome us.

"Mrs. Eliza," Michaela said, "I haven't seen you in a long time, it must be a whole year already," she smiled. Michaela and my mother had liked each other instantly when they met, and I had almost forgotten how much.

"Michaela, you haven't changed one bit," my mother smiled and hugged her. My mother and Michaela had only met each other the time my mother had come to stay with us, and yet they seemed to have managed to get closer to each other than my mother and I had been able to get.

My mother was the kind of woman who always lived every moment to the fullest, no matter how hard her life was, she always seemed to find reasons to be happy. Obviously, I didn't inherit that quality from her.

"Mom, let's go upstairs, get some rest, freshen up, and then we'll take a walk," I interrupted them.

"Okay, let's," she agreed, and I took her things.

"Mr. Arthur told me that Mrs. Eliza was coming, so I immediately prepared the guest room," Michaela said.

"Alright, thank you," I called out.

"Arthur is so nice. He thinks of everything," said my mother, and I tried to keep quiet, even though I wanted to turn around and ask her, 'What Arthur are we talking about, Mom?'

I set her bags down in the guest room and asked her if she would be alright.

"I'll be great, I'm comfortable in this room, I slept here on my last visit," she smiled. "I'm leaving on Tuesday," and as she said it she sat down on the bed. "Sit down," she said, patting the spot beside her to indicate where I should sit, "let me see your eyes."

I didn't sit down beside her.

"I know you didn't enjoy your last visit to Roubaix. We quarreled and I may have overreacted. I never told you, but now I'm telling you. My intention was never to hurt you, but to awaken you."

"Awaken me?" I was perplexed, and sat down where she had pointed.

"Yes. From a young age you were a sad child, a beautiful doll with long ginger hair and big green eyes, who seemed to be waiting for someone to scold you so that you could cry out loud. You were always the same as your father, that's why you got along with him so well. You two sat together and talked about life, the things that disappointed you, the injustices, the bad people, and the heartache. After he died you didn't only lose your father, you also lost the only person who really understood you. I know that, that's why his death left such a lasting mark on you. Your father always thought that he was a deep man because he could talk about the meaning of life. I'm different, I may not have been able to communicate with you but I fought for our livelihood every day.WhenI worked in the factory, I worked happily until the day of my retirement. No matter what, I was always motivated to get out and be busy," and as she spoke she started to tremble a little and cry.

"Mom," I grabbed her hand.

"Margot, all I wanted was for you to take after me just a little bit. I wanted you to understand my simplicity, and to be less impressed and inspired by your father's deep, philosophical ways. Most of all, I wanted you to be happy. No one should live in anger and rage, no one should be proud of being disappointed. It doesn't make a person smart to be like that, it makes a person incredibly defeated. I didn't want you to be defeated. I didn't want you to wake up one day and realize you missed out on many things. Life is hard, I know, but my lovely Margot, it is also so beautiful."

"Mom, please stop," I began to shake a little.

"Please, I want to say everything."

"Margot, I know your father's death makes you think you should have a baby as soon as possible, but that's not the case. Do you think that happiness is tied to becoming a mother? Yes, that's wonderful if it happens, but it doesn't mean you'll automatically be happy. Happiness is something else, my daughter. Happiness is in everyday life, in small things. I'm scared, I'm scared by your constant dissatisfaction and the sadness in your eyes that's become so pleasant to you. I think you forget how dangerous it is," she said, still trembling and crying harder.

I hugged her tightly and we didn't let go of each other. My mother never spoke like this, I thought. I didn't know that she could speak like this.

"Margot," she said, loosening herself from my arms, "if you aren't discovering something new every day, then you're not living, you're just existing. Do you understand? I can't forget how proud I was when you graduated as a sociologist. You were one of the top students in your class, and then what happened? You couldn't find a job because you didn't like the way the system worked. You got disappointed and gave up and didn't even try. Your father understood you, of course your father understood you. I never understood you. I still don't understand you. Margot, don't you understand that you have to build your own system?"

She looked at me and I stroked her hair. She had the softest, short brown hair and deep brown eyes. I could smell her perfume. She wore the same scent for as long as I could remember. It was sweet-smelling, just like vanilla. She bought it from a cheap store in Roubaix after a lady who worked there told her that all the elegant ladies smelled like vanilla. She always bought the same scent and every time she would hug me, I thought I would faint from the strong whiff. Vanilla always reminded me of my mother.

I hugged her again and my tears started to flow. I knew my mother had wanted me to open up emotionally for a long time. I cried and couldn't calm down. Maybe we had to cry together to start laughing together. Maybe this is something we were both waiting for.

"Mom, I don't want our day to end like this."

"The day is beautiful, don't worry."

We wiped the tears from our faces, then smiled, and laughed.

"Mom, I can't stop laughing," I shouted, giggling between drying tears.

"Neither can I," she giggled like never before, and in that moment I knew - I will always remember this.

I went to my room to lie down, stretching my arms to get the knots out of my upper back. I closed my eyes, tried to think of nothing, and fell asleep. A little later my phone rang, waking me up, and I got out of bed and took it out of my bag. I saw your name, Arthur.

"Margot, how are you? Did Eliza come? Is everything okay?"

"Yes, everything is fine, we're at home," I said.

"Earlier my mother and I decided we would go for a walk at the Champs Elysees after we rested a bit, and then we'd have lunch or dinner somewhere," I said, telling you about our plans.

"Great," you said, "can I join you two? Not for the walk, I mean for lunch or dinner."

I was surprised by that. You were never worried about how we looked in my mother's eyes, so I knew that you didn't want to join us for that reason. On the other hand, I couldn't believe that the answer might simply be that you wanted to spend time with your wife and her mother. I never thought the solution could be that obvious, but after talking to my mother I began to think that perhaps the absolute depth of a person lies in their simplicity.

"Margot?"

"Yes, of course Arthur," I replied, coming back to the conversation.

"Tell me where you plan to eat and I'll meet you there."

After you hung up, I lowered the phone to my chest and held it against my heart. My pulse was racing incredibly fast. I decided I wanted to dress up because I wanted to look beautiful for you. I chose a nice white pants and a matching white shirt. I looked in the mirror and decided I needed red lipstick. As I was putting on the lipstick, I started to remember how we had met. You came to Roubaix for work and saw me in a café one evening. I was sitting at a table with my friend Pierre, and we were chatting and laughing. You were sitting two tables to the left of us and didn't take your eyes off me, trying to catch my attention. I would look at you from time to time, but I didn't think you were seriously interested in talking to me. I thought you were just a flirt. The waiter brought over two drinks, one for me and one for Pierre, and said it was from the gentleman sitting two tables away from us. I knew I liked you because you had included Pierre, and I also knew that you were smart, because you obviously didn't think that he was a threat to you. After a while, we were all sitting together - you, me, and Pierre. He didn't stop kicking me under the table. We both fell in love with you that night and you fell in love with me. After just a few weeks you wanted to spend your life with me, and I never doubted my feelings. I hadn't thought back to how we'd met in quite some time and it was nice to remember it now I thought, as I checked my outfit in the mirror.

I went to call my mother, but she wasn't in the guest room. I found her sitting in the kitchen with Michaela, chatting, while Michaela was washing the dishes.

"Mom, are you ready?"

"Margot, how beautiful you look, my daughter, you are a real Parisian woman," she smiled. "Isn't it true, Michaela?"

"She is most beautiful," Michaela said.

"Stop it, you'll embarrass me." I turned to Michaela and said, "We're going out for a walk, see you tomorrow."

"Have a nice time!"

"Let's go by car, Mom," I suggested.

"But it's not that far, is it?"

"No, less than three kilometers, but we'll walk when we get there too and I don't want you to get tired," I explained.

"You're right," she said as we left home, "sometimes that quality of yours is handy," she pinched my hand.

"Which quality is that?"

I opened the car door.

"I don't know its name," she sighed. "You have some kind of a need to take life and squeeze all the air out of it."

"Okay then," I said, not wanting to get into further discussion, especially since I knew my mother was telling the truth.

I thought I couldn't wait to start talking to her about the beautiful things happening inside me, about the charity I joined, about my new daily routine, and the life that I'm changing - but at the same time it was hard for me to talk to her about it.

As we drove, I realized that I only spoke to my mother about bad things. I talk about things that are wrong, about negative people, about problems in society, about what's missing. I really don't know how to start a conversation and say that I'm fine and that I'm happy, that my life is beautiful, and that good things are happening. I don't know how to do it without feeling out of place. Maybe my sorrow has grown on me like it's something pleasant, and I really don't know if I'll be able to get used to happiness and stop being uncomfortable with it.

Looking out of the window my mother said, "Margot, Paris is a beautiful city, isn't it?"

"Yes," I said.

"Let's buy hats," she said.

"Hats?"

"Yes, some nice hats. We can wear them in the sun."

"Maybe.There are a lot of shops on the Champs Elysees,

we'll find something for sure," I smiled.

"Great," she shouted like a small child. I felt at ease with her and comfortable in my own skin.

My mother and I parked the car and walked hand in hand. The Champs Elysees was crowded, as always. There were people everywhere, walking, taking pictures, and shopping. I felt euphoric.

"There are too many people here," my mother said.

"Yes, it's always like that here."

"Mom, I want to tell you something," I began.

"Yes," she said.

"Some time ago, I was determined to leave Arthur," I barely managed to say the sentence, and my mother paused.

"And?"

I looked down and said, "I wanted to leave him because I was incredibly unhappy. When we couldn't have a baby, I lost control of my emotions. I had so many plans and nothing worked out the way I wanted it to. Arthur worked so much, Mom. He spent all day at SFR, I was alone, and when he got home from work, I was angry and he was tired. We stopped talking, we forgot how to be with each other. We turned into strangers who share a house, but fall asleep separately. It was very difficult for me. I was determined to leave him and start over, but I found a new perspective and that gradually took me in a different direction. I listened to stories about other people's hardships, and was able to see things from a different angle. I started to focus on myself, I tried to make my own days more enjoyable, and worked on finding happiness in little things."

My mother put her hand on my shoulder to comfort me. Her touch was soft, and I continued explaining.

"I volunteer at a charity now. I'm helping them with their work - to give assistance to parents of new babies, parents who are struggling. When I did that, my days started to change, and so did my life. I think Arthur notices that there have been positive changes within me and maybe that makes him happy. That's great and I'm glad about it, but it's not the point of what I'm doing. My focus is on myself now. I'm trying to be a better person. I got rid of a lot of anger and rage. I still don't really know what will happen to my marriage, but I've found some peace now, Mom. I don't know if you know what I mean," as I finished my sentence I lifted my head to meet her eyes.

"Margot, I understand you better than you think," she said, her gaze fixed on me.

We had stopped walking and were facing each other.

"Life is not about being disappointed and wondering how it could be if things were different," she said. "No, that is a waste of time, but you have to take what you were given and make it as good as you can. I know it's not easy, especially for us women. I'm talking about all the stereotypes, prejudices, and expectations in the world, and what is expected of us and how we're supposed to endure it in the name of being a good woman. Listen to me Margot, it doesn't have to be like that for you. You can build your own beautiful little world within this vast and empty universe. You do what you want. Do you remember what I said to you before you left for Paris?"

I had completely forgotten that we were on the Champs Elysees and I didn't pay attention to anything around me, I was fully focused on our conversation.

"What did you say?" I asked. I wanted to hear it once more, although I remembered it very well.

"Go and make your life beautiful."

"Yes, but isn't life beautiful by itself?"

"True, but we humans have the incredible power to destroy it, not grasping how beautiful life really is," she said. "We have the power to do what we want with life. Somewhere it may be written that Margot should be happy, but if Margot doesn't want it, it won't be. Somewhere it may be written that Margot deserves to be successful, but if Margot doesn't want it, it won't happen. What can life do when Margot decides to do nothing? What? You see, life can't save you when you don't want to save yourself," she sighed. "I don't want to tell you anything else, I know very well that marriage is not an easy thing. I will only tell you that if someone prevents you from being happy, then that is reason enough for you to leave, but if you prevent yourself from being happy," then that is reason enough to change," she smiled.

"Yes," I said, understanding what she meant.

"I told you this morning too, becoming a mother is wonderful, but that doesn't mean you'll definitely be happy. Not having a baby isn't your problem. Your problem is elsewhere, my daughter. I just want you to be happy and at peace with yourself. I wish that for you. I'm proud of you for discovering new things. Give yourself a chance, I hope you know that you deserve countless chances, and you deserve the best kind of love too," she stroked my face.

"Did you give Dad chances?"

"He gave them to me and I gave them to him, every day," her eyes watered, and so did mine.

I felt light and hugged my mother. I just had the instinct to hold her. I don't remember the last time I talked to her like this, I didn't know that she knew me so well. I had been locked inside myself for so long, convinced that I knew absolutely everything. I was wrong.

"I love you," I said.

"Always," she replied.

We hugged for a few minutes and maybe to all the people passing by it was a normal day, but my mother and I knew it was a special day.

"Are we crying again, and next we will laugh?"

She smiled and wiped away my tears, and I wiped away hers.

"We have the whole day to laugh," I said feeling happy, "are we going to look for hats?"

"Let's go!"

We started walking again, looking into shop windows as we walked by, and I waited for her to make a suggestion on where to go next. It was a lovely walk and we enjoyed ourselves.

"Let's go here, maybe they have hats," she said, pointing at Gallery Lafayette.

"Maybe they do."

"Margot, this is wonderful, tell me, have I been here before? I can't remember."

"Not with me, I haven't brought you here."

"So I haven't been here then."

"I must have told you about Gallery Lafayette? It's one of the best places in Paris to shop."

"Maybe you did. I can't recall."

We went inside and I remembered the first time I came here with you, Arthur. I'd always wanted to come here, but I never thought I'd get to do it with the love of my life. I hardly believed in anything before I met you, but then you came along and changed that. You were like a fairytale that became reality, and I wanted it, I wanted the fairytale to be true.

"Margot, it's magical," my mother said.

"It really is."

"Let's take a walk and see what they've got over there, we can look around and find nice hats," she pulled me forward by my hand.

"Margot, over here everything is only for women."

"Yes, there's a separate building for men."

"Finally something just for us," she smiled. "Let's separate and see who finds the best hats," she said, and left.

"Be careful," I called after her and started window shopping. It had been a while since I came here. In fact, it had been a while since I enjoyed Paris. Arthur, you bought my red dress here, the one I wore the other night when I wanted to surprise you on our anniversary. Unfortunately, that date ended badly, but that dress holds another wonderful memory for me. When you gave it to me, I wore it to out to dinner with you - it was just the two of us, and afterward we went for a lovely walk through Paris. I never wore it again until the night I made you the spaghetti. I thought if I put it on it would be like the old days again, but the dress wasn't enough. I don't know if anything will be enough.

"Margot, look," I heard my mother's voice behind me and I turned around. She wore a large, dark blue hat on her head. "Do you like it? I know you like this color."

"It's beautiful," I smiled, "you look great, is there one for me?"

She had another one in her hand and I took it.

"Yes, let's buy them, they're on sale."

"You always knew how to find good deals."

"I know exactly what I want and I don't stop until I find it."

As she said that I had the feeling she was alluding to something else. Walking behind her, I thought, 'Am I really a person who doesn't know what she wants? Is that the root of my problems?' It bothered me, so I asked her, "Mom, have I always been like this?".

She was looking at another hat.

"This one?"

"Do I not know what I want?" I repeated.

"I would rather say that you're afraid to love, but that's understandable. Living in darkness all of your life, I'm not surprised that every little light scares you."

"Darkness? What do you mean?"

"Margot, you didn't become unhappy in Paris. You've always been like that. You just forgot, as you always forget and then blame others for your misery. That was the main problem in our relationship, and in my relationship with your father too. Unfortunately, you inherited that from him."

"Mom, you're insulting me and we'll end up fighting again."

"Well, it won't be the first time, but I think you should hear the truth. You must!"

"Stop it!" I shouted at her.

"Was it really so hard to learn to be happy here? Was it

really so difficult to get used to a different life, to try something new, and to grow up?"

"Mom, I told you, I've been trying. It's not easy!"

"I know it's not easy, my daughter, because you make it difficult! Happiness is your obligation my dear, just like breathing! You have to be happy, you owe it to yourself because you need it to survive!"

She shouted louder, and I noticed that people were looking at us.

"I'm leaving!" I said.

I turned around and almost started running. I left my mother in the mall alone and drove all the way home without her. I didn't go back for her. She always knows how to hurt me the most, it almost seems intentional. I'm sure she came to Paris to ruin the great mood I had. We've struggled like this all my life. I've tried to find a way to talk to her without it ending in a fight. Nothing has changed.

When I got home there was no one there and I felt terrible. I didn't want to call you or anyone. I went to our bedroom, changed my clothes and put my head down on the pillow, closing my eyes. I was trying to breathe and not think too much. Unintentionally, I fell asleep.

"Margot, wake up," I heard your voice.

I woke up and didn't know where I was. I saw you sitting on the bed next to me, wearing a t-shirt and athletic pants. I didn't know where to begin explaining.

"I fell asleep," I said, coming to my senses. "My mother, where is my mother, Arthur? I left her, I left her in the mall, at Gallery Lafayette! Arthur, we have to go fetch her, she's alone," I shouted uncontrollably and started crying.

"Margot," you tried to speak.

"Arthur, you don't understand me! You never understand me!" I started hitting you. "We have to go and find my mother, I left her alone!" I repeated desperately.

"Margot!" You shouted and held my hands to keep them still, "Margot, your mother is here, and she is fine."

I looked at you confused. "She's here?"

"She's here, I picked her up, we had lunch together and we came back. We've been at home for some time. I didn't want to wake you up right away. Your mother was tired and fell asleep," you explained.

"You had lunch together?" I was furious.

"Yes, we were hungry."

"So my mother comes to Paris to spend time with you and to have lunch with you. How did that happen Arthur, how is that possible?"

Tears came running down my face.

"Well, it is possible. You left your mother in a huge mall alone, and because she doesn't know anyone else in Paris, and she knows you very well and knows that you won't come back for her, she called me. In the meantime, we got hungry and sat down to lunch. What don't you understand?" It seemed like you were scolding me.

"You turned out to be a real hero then. Bravo! Now you can tell me how I'm supposed to treat my mother. Who are you to tell me? You don't have your own parents, now you want to take my mother from me. You took everything from me but it's still not enough for you!"

"Yes, my parents died and that's why I don't have them with me anymore. Your mother is alive, if that means anything to you. I don't want to take your mother from you, just as I don't want to take anything from you. On the contrary, I'm trying to give you something. Unfortunately, that can't happen by force," you said and walked away from the bed.

"Where are you going?" I shouted

"I'm going downstairs to the living room. I'm sleeping there, you sleep here. I hope you have a good night's rest and let your mother rest too. Tomorrow is a new day, if you even care," you said, leaving the room.

"I do care,"I said softly to myself, feeling ashamed.

"Margot, you should apologize to her," you said as you turned to face me.

I said nothing.

"As for me, you don't have to apologize to me. I think you've imagined yourself to be the eternal victim. I won't spoil it for you. Good night," you said and went out and closed the door, leaving me in an empty room full of questions.

I didn't dare to leave the room. I didn't dare to say another word. I grabbed a sheet of paper and a pen, just as rage had grabbed my soul earlier that day. I started writing and the conversation with myself untangled my tangled threads.

Yours,

Margot

P.S. I must accept this demon that lives inside me, because this demon will always be part of me. I know the demon will never leave me. Does that mean one of us must die? I can't run away from the demon without running away from the truth - the demon is not external to me - I am the demon and the demon is me.

CHAPTER FOURTEEN

August 19, 2019

My dear Arthur,

Today was one of those days I really didn't know how to behave. I felt that I lost even the small bit of direction I had managed to find. I woke up early but I didn't have the courage to leave the room. After a while I heard your voice and my mother's voice. You talked and laughed as if nothing had happened. I felt that life goes on and it was only my life that stood still. I really don't know why I'm still in a maze and it seems I can't get out of it. My daily confession on blank sheets of paper gives me some guidance, yet I'm still confused. I try to be honest with myself but it's difficult for me to learn to live differently. I've been focusing on everything I've missed out on for so long. It was a habit of negativity that was of course very dangerous. Certain habits enslave a person and prevent you from making progress.

I'm beginning to understand why you're so successful Arthur. Progress is the most important thing to you, and with every success you want new success. If I put myself in your shoes, I can imagine how you must have felt when you came home from work daily. You probably looked at me, completely the same every day, sitting there like I was frozen with anger and rage, while you wanted to move forward. It is certainly not easy to love a woman who doesn't love herself at all.

After I woke up, I mustered enough courage to go downstairs. I wanted to see you before Michaela came in.

"Good morning," I said, and you and my mother looked at me in surprise as you sat in the living room drinking coffee.

"Good morning, my dear child," my mother said.

"How are you, Margot? Do you want coffee?"

"I'm fine," I smiled, because you made me feel welcomed. "I do, but I'll make my own cup," I said and headed for the kitchen.

"Arthur and I are laughing, we were recalling the moment we met," my mother said. "Do you remember how scared he was?"

My mother laughed out loud.

"Scared?" I asked, pouring water into the kettle.

"Yes, his hands were shaking," she laughed.

"I don't remember him being like that."

"I was scared, you just didn't see it."

"Maybe," I sighed and sat down on the sofa, sipping from my mug.

"Oh this coffee is so nice," I sighed.

You asked me what my mother and I were planning for the day, and you said that you have a project to finish for work, but that you'd be free to join us for lunch in two or three hours.

"Alright," I said.

"Sounds nice," my mother agreed.

We knew we needed to talk.

"Okay, then," you said, "talk to you two later," you got up and went upstairs to the bedroom to get ready for work.

My mother and I remained sitting in the living room.

"Will Michaela come in today?"

"Yes. She's coming in," I said.

After a moment's silence I spoke again.

"Mom, I want to talk to you about yesterday," I pulled together enough courage to say.

"Margot, you really shouldn't. You're my child. I love you, you don't need to explain anything to me. "Really," she looked at me with tears in her eyes.

"That's not enough. I know you love me but that doesn't

mean I shouldn't explain my actions to you. I'll start at the beginning. You know that I'm going through a rough period and I'm trying to find my way. I'm sure you noticed Arthur and I aren't sleeping in the same bed. I don't want to pretend to be someone else around you. I don't know how to tell you this Mom, and I don't want to hurt you, but you often make me feel like I'm a bad person. Every time we see each other you remind me of all the things I've done that you don't approve of, and that really blocks me from moving forward. We've always had that problem because you love to criticize me. It was easier with Dad. Dad accepted me as I am. He would hear me out, I could talk to him," I said, trying to find the right words.

"Margot," my mother said, but I interrupted her.

"I'm not done," I said, "let me finish what I have to say before Arthur comes back down."

"Arthur won't come down at the wrong time, believe me," she said.

"Okay, you know best," I said sarcastically and relented.

"Margot, this isn't about me. It's about you. I know everything was different with your father. Yes, your father always had time to talk to you, because he wasn't as busy as I was - he didn't have a permanent job to hold down like I did. He worked, but hopped from one job to the next. He was always dissatisfied and always said he was waiting for his chance. And so, life passed. And me? I lived that boring life, I went to work every day, I tried to earn money and contribute to our upkeep, taking care of all of us. I didn't want you to get used to talking about how unfair life is. I wanted you to be able to see all the opportunities that life has to offer," my mother said, then paused and continued again. "I don't know, maybe I was too strict on you. Maybe I should have been different, but I was happy when Arthur came into your life. I thought - this is the male figure you need, but here you are again, at the same point, just in a completely different place. You can physically escape from things but never from yourself. You dragged your imaginary problems into your new life, overestimated yourself, thought that you'd be able to carry them and still live normally, but they knocked you down to the ground, covered you, and now you can hardly breathe. Am I right?"

At that moment Arthur, you and Michaela both arrived.

As you bumped into her you said, "Michaela, you're here?"

"Yes," she replied with a laugh.

"I'm going now, I'll see you later. Have a nice day ladies," you called out, and from the way you looked at me I knew you were clear about how you felt. It was as if you were saying to me, 'Margot, you can do this.' Strange as it seems, I'm beginning to think you know me better than I thought.

"Mrs. Eliza, how are you?" Michaela said.

"I'm fine," my mother smiled and got up.

"What are the plans for today?" Michaela asked.

"Nothing, we're going to have lunch with Arthur later, and now we're going to get some rest," my mother explained.

"Yes?" I looked at her.

"Well, yes," she said.

"Good," I said.

Michaela asked if she should make us a nice, tasty breakfast.

"Yes," said my mother, and took my hand. "Will you come upstairs with me? I want to show you something."

I wondered what it was as we made our way to the guest room. As we walked upstairs my mother said that her head hurt.

"Would you like me to get you a pill?"

"No, never mind, there's no cure for this," she said as she entered the room.

"What do you mean there's no cure?" I was worried by her choice of words.

"No, I just misspoke," she smiled and sat down on the bed, taking a deep breath, "I mean there's no cure for a good old headache. I've always suffered from headaches, you know."

"Yes, from fatigue when you worked, but what's this from?"

"Margot, everything is fine. Actually, do you see that bag over there, do you see it? I want you to take out what's in it," she pointed at the bag, holding her other hand over her stomach.

"Does your stomach hurt?" I asked anxiously, walking toward the bag.

"No, no, everything is fine, please," she smiled.

I picked up the bag and sat down next to her on the bed.

"What's this?"

"A photo album. Open it," she said, stroking my hair.

I opened the album and the first picture I saw was of me.

"How old am I here?" I was surprised to see these old pictures of me.

"Only three," she said.

"I have long hair here too," I smiled.

"You have always had beautiful, long, ginger hair. You looked so much like your father. You still do," she said, continuing to stroke it.

"And this one? Where does this picture come from?"

"This was taken the day you learned to swim at Camping Bel Sito. We camped there every year for I don't know how long, it was really very beautiful," she smiled.

"Yes, I remember we did."

"And this one?" I asked.

"This picture is from there too. All our summer vacations were there. We went there until you turned thirteen," she sighed.

"And then?"

"Then we stopped," she shrugged.

"Why?"

"Your father started to dislike camping and we had no money for anything else. You grew up, you began to understand, and you usually agreed with him. Two against one."

"Yes, I remember," I was a bit embarrassed, and kept looking at the photos. "So Dad didn't want to go to the beach anymore?"

"No, it wasn't about that. Your father didn't want to live life. Nothing was enough for him and on the other hand he didn't aim to have anything more. He was always the king of our family and I still respect that. I'm not surprised that he won your heart, but I'm sad because you repeat some of his mistakes and you feel the consequences in your own life," she said quietly.

"Maybe it's easier for me that way."

"Maybe."

"And this one? I know. This is my sixteenth birthday with the three of us. I remember this day," I smiled.

"Yes, I took this photo of you and your father, it was his favorite photograph. He put it in that frame he made himself, like a box that opens. I told him that frame was a very clever idea and that he should start selling them, but he didn't want to. He gave up without even trying. That's what he was like. Capable, but didn't want responsibility. When he died, you didn't separate yourself from that frame."

"Yes, I even brought it here with me," I said. "You remember, don't you?"

"Yes, yes," my mother replied, but answered as if she were far away.

"Beautiful memories,"I said.

"Yes, but it's time for new memories, don't you agree?"

She took the album from my hand and set it aside.

"I agree," I said.

She gripped my hand incredibly tightly and said, "That's life my dear!" She tried to hide the tears that flowed from her eyes by hugging me.

"Life?" I hugged her back even harder.

"Yes, life - beautiful, just beautiful," she smiled heroically, "shall we go have breakfast?"

"Yes, come on, and after breakfast we can take a walk, just around the neighborhood."

"And then we'll call Arthur for lunch," she smiled, "this

time, for real."

"This time for real," I smiled.

We hugged hard once more. I knew then that I was lucky to have my mother, and just because we had fights with each other, it didn't mean we couldn't be close.

"Eggs, how wonderful," my mother said when she saw the breakfast Michaela had prepared for us.

The special connection my mother and Michaela seemed to have bothered me at first - I don't know why. I even brought it up in arguments with my mother. I remember telling her, 'I know you want me to be like Michaela, I know you'd like me to be like her.' My mother laughed at that and told me I was crazy. She said I was incredibly talented at finding problems where no one else could find them. When Michaela was telling me her life story, I remembered how my mother and I had argued about her, and I felt very ashamed of myself for how I had acted then. At the end of the day, there is nothing wrong with my mother wanting me to be at least a little bit like Michaela, I said to myself, after all, she is a brave and beautiful woman. We thanked Michaela for the meal and began to eat.

My mother said, "It tastes good, doesn't it?"

"Yes, it's delicious," I said.

"Michaela, do you know what?" My mother looked at me, glowing as she spoke. "When Margot was a child, she suddenly didn't want to eat eggs anymore. Every day I tried to get her to try them but she refused. She said she didn't want to eat eggs and that it was her decision. One day, I made eggs like this in a small casserole dish and told her they were melted biscuits. She ate them and loved them. I knew from then onwards Margot was going to be a challenge, but if I could find a way to tame her, it might just be the easiest thing to raise her," my mother said, and I couldn't stop laughing.

"That's one of my favorite stories. It really is," I said, and Michaela laughed too.

"That's how it is, my dear, so find a way to tame yourself then it will be easier for you." I actually understood exactly what my mother meant by that.

After breakfast we went for our walk. The weather outside was nice, there was a gentle breeze that made August more beautiful. We strolled through the neighborhood hand in hand. My mother was more quiet than usual. I thought something was wrong but I didn't want to say anything. I was trying to be more sensitive than I usually was.

"It's nice here," she said suddenly.

"Yes," I sighed.

"I really like walking, it calms me down. Your father didn't like it, for him it was a waste of time."

"Mom, I want to ask you something."

"Ask me, Margot."

"Why didn't you leave Dad, if he really was the way you say he was? When I hear you talk, it seems the two of you were really different from each other. Why did you stay with him?"

"Margot, I didn't leave your father because I loved him. He wasn't a bad person, he simply looked at the world in a different way than I did. His faults came from not knowing how to live differently. I built my own life and my own daily routine and he didn't hold me back from that. Instead of longing for everything I wanted to do with him, I found things I could do for myself. I had my work, knitting, home - I found happiness this way. Sometimes the people we fall in love with are people who, if we meet them again - we would have nothing to talk about, but the love doesn't disappear. Love is always there for the ones who know that they shouldn't expect their partners to make them happy. Love is always enough," she said. "The person who truly understands love doesn't suffocate it with expectations but leaves it to be what it is. Love is an amazing gift. Don't forget Margot, love never leaves the home first, it's people who do that. The same people who justify their mistakes with the absence of love, but in fact it's us - we decide when love fades. Love is powerful but it doesn't disappear on its own. It's not as complex as people say it is. Love is the simplest thing in the world," my mother said, as she stroked my hair.

I listened to her talk, and thought she was very wise. All my life I'd been walking around with my deep soul, not thinking that the deepest souls are the hidden ones. I decided not to say anything more, in fact I didn't know what more to say. We kept walking until we reached the beautiful gardens of Trocadero. I simply wanted to enjoy my mother's presence.

"This is one of my favorite places in Paris," I said.

"Because of the Tower?"

"No, because I love gardens. I think the Tower is overrated."

"When you were little you dreamed of coming to Paris and seeing the Eiffel Tower. Now you live very close to it, but you think it's overrated."

"Now I dream of other things," I said.

"That's good, but it doesn't mean that old dreams should be forgotten. They are very important for you to appreciate how happy you really are."

We walked further but didn't say much after that. About an hour and a half later, my mother suggested we call you, Arthur, and go to lunch. She had to travel back to Roubaix the next day, and wanted to get home early so she could rest. She didn't want to stay out all day. I agreed and called you.

"Arthur, we're at the gardens of Trocadero. My mother wants to have lunch now," I said, talking to you over the phone.

"I can be there in twenty minutes, at most half an hour," you said. "Where do you want to have lunch?"

"I don'tknow, what do you think about LeCoq? We're near there."

"Can you get us a table? I'll be there soon. Kisses, Margot," you said hurriedly and hung up.

Your last two words took me by surprise. I must have been smiling because my mother asked me why I looked so happy.

"What?" I replied.

"What are you smiling about, darling? Did Arthur say something?"

"No, no,"I said, feeling a bit embarrassed. "I'm not smiling, Mom, everything is fine."

"You know, it's okay to smile when you talk to your husband, because even though you have problems, you can admit you love him," she pinched my cheek.

"Mom, let's go to the restaurant," I changed the subject, "it's very close, just a right here, then right again, and then we're there. Arthur will meet us as soon as he can."

At the restaurant my mother went to the ladies' room while I waited at our table, my head spinning with thoughts. I was replaying that scene where you sent me kisses over the phone, over and over in my head. My heart triggered an unreserved smile, but I wasn't sure if that meant I was happy.

Coming back from the bathroom, my mother said, "This place is so elegant, just look at the velvet chairs, so nice. Margot, did you order yet?"

She always seemed like she was so happy and full of energy. I envied that.

"No, not yet," I replied.

"Let's have a glass of champagne, what do you say, to celebrate your birthday?"

"Mom, forget about the birthday, it's not important. There'll be many other birthdays."

She went quiet and I felt bad.

"Sorry," I said,"I know you look forward to every birthday I have. Let's drink some champagne."

I had just said that and then I heard your voice say, "I didn't miss anything did I?"

I looked up and saw that you had suddenly appeared Arthur. I felt self-conscious suddenly, and avoided eye contact with you.

"Arthur! Hello," my mother exclaimed. "Sit down, sit next to Margot. I want to see you two sitting next to each other," she said, and you, though clearly uncertain, sat down next to me.

"How are you? Did you order? I'm a little earlier than I said I would be."

You were nervous. I was nervous too. Our bodies weren't touching but the scent of your aftershave lingered around me, and I could hear you take a deep breath, as if you needed more air.

"Today we're drinking champagne to celebrate Margot's birthday," my mother said.

"Great," you said and called the waiter. While you were ordering I started sweating. I felt like I was sinking into deep water and something seemed to be pulling me down. I couldn't sit still. My vision became hazy. My mother's face looked completely different to me and her laughter sounded distant, like we weren't sitting at the same table. I felt the impulse to crack my knuckles, to shift around from left to right, and to fidget. You appeared to be calm and smiling - and that upset me even more. I gathered my hair together with a pin, but my head hurt, so I let it loose again.

"Margot, you're beautiful," said my mother, noticing my discomfort, and she put her hand on mine.

"I'm sweaty," I said, pulling my hand back, not wanting you to notice how nervous I was, Arthur.

You turned to my mother and said, "Sweaty? It's not that hot in here is it? It's really nice actually."

"It's perfect for me," my mother smiled.

"That's great, Mom, but it's not perfect for me," I said anxiously.

"Margot, please, don't do this," my mother said, reacting to my tone.

"I'm not doing anything!" I shouted, as the waiter came with our champagne.

While you were talking to him about the champagne, my

mother shot me an icy stare.

"Margot, we won't have a chance like this again, please, don't be difficult. Relax, everything is fine," she said with a little smile, expecting me to smile back at her, but I found her tone condescending.

"Mom, what do you mean by that? Are you saying that you came here for me and that you won't do it again because I don't deserve it? Or maybe you're trying to say that my behavior is strange? I agree, it really is, isn't it? We're sitting together as if everything is fine. My mother is sitting opposite me, and we can barely talk, and my husband is sitting beside me, and we have a terrible marriage. Great, really wonderful!" I shouted, and the waiter quickly poured our glasses and disappeared from the table.

You gave me a look Arthur, and said, "Margot, you're making a scene and you've got it all wrong!" You looked at my mother who was silent, holding her head with her hands.

"I see that you two understand each other very well, so I'll leave you alone. Yesterday you had the opportunity to talk, and now you'll have the opportunity to continue. Thank you for the birthday surprise, but I really don't need such fake ceremonies!" I shouted and got up from the table.

"Margot," my mother began to cry, holding my hand.

"Mom, you may think you're this great woman who managed to live with a man who was different from you, but it's clear to me that there's nothing great about that. Great people don't suffer such a life, great people deserve great happiness!"

I pulled my hand away from hers and left.

I left the restaurant and it didn't take me more than two minutes to feel ashamed of myself. Deep down I didn't believe any of the words I had said. My demon had defeated me once more, and I had lied to myself again, thinking that the demon was someone other than me.

I walked the streets of our neighborhood for a few more

hours. I didn't know where I was going but I didn't want to stop. I wanted to get tired enough so that I could fall asleep easily. My thoughts were chewing at me from everywhere and my conscience swallowed me in one bite. I felt guilty but also helpless. I always thought I'd be able to jump from one story to another, but I seem to have stuck to this sad story for too long. This seems to be the only way I know how to be and I'm not sure I know how to be any other way. I used to think that I was incredibly brave because I could shout and leave when I wanted to, but I've come to see that that's not courage at all.

When I got home I didn't see Michaela so I assumed she had left. Going upstairs, I noticed the guest bedroom was locked and I didn't even try to go inside. I went into our bedroom and saw you lying on the bed with your eyes and your arms wide open.

"Arthur, what are you doing?"

You sighed and got off the bed. You walked past me to leave the room, then turned and looked at me.

"No Margot, what are you doing?"

You turned again to go toward the door, and left. I didn't try to stop you. I didn't try to say anything. I stripped down completely naked, went to lie down, and covered myself with the bedsheet and nothing more. I couldn't bear anything on my skin because of the guilt burning me. I could smell you, my disappointment, and my anger. I tried to find an excuse for my behavior, but I couldn't.

I started writing this, and while writing I witnessed how my world was collapsing. No, I have no right to say that. My world isn't collapsing. I am destroying my world.

Yours,

Margot

P.S. I don't know how to change what hurts me the most. After all the things my mother told me about my father I'm sure

119

she knew I'd ask her why she didn't leave him. I'm sure she wanted to give me an answer which would help me look at my own marriage differently. I'm still asking the obvious questions. It hurts me that I don't change and that I seem unable to get out of this skin. I don't grow. It's very sad Arthur, it's infinitely and endlessly sad that years have passed and I'm still angry about the same things. I want to give up the anger. I want to finally grasp that even when it's very difficult it doesn't necessarily mean that it's someone's fault.

CHAPTER FIFTEEN

August 20, 2019

My dear Arthur,

Today I returned to my old habits. I got up late and didn't want to get out of bed. I lost all desire to do anything. I felt as if I had no strength at all and as if I didn't know what to do with myself.

At about eleven o'clock I stepped out of the bedroom and could barely get down the stairs. Michaela greeted me with a worried look. I told her I was fine, feeling the need to defend myself although she didn't attack me.

"Where is my mother?"

She asked me what I meant and then asked if I wanted coffee, changing the subject.

"Where is my mother? Can you answer that simple question?"

"Margot, Mrs. Eliza left early this morning. Arthur took her to the train station. I bumped into him this morning when I arrived and he told me." She was almost inaudible as she told me.

"Did my mother leave without saying goodbye to me?"

"I don't know Margot, I really don't know and I don't want to interfere," she said in a scared tone.

"I don't need coffee, I don't need anything," I got up from my chair and went back into the bedroom. I slammed the door and sat on the bed. I started squeezing my head with both my hands. I didn't know how to stop the pain I was feeling inside. I couldn't stand it and I called you.

"Yes, Margot," you said answering the phone.

"Arthur, I heard you took my mother to the train station and she left," I said nervously.

"Yes, early this morning," you replied, as if there was no problem.

"Why did you take her?"

"Should I have let her go alone?"

"I really don't understand how you could do that while I was sleeping. Why didn't anyone wake me up, why didn't anyone tell me anything?"

"Margot, stop yelling," you said. "You knew that your mother was planning to leave early this morning and you didn't get up to see her off, that was your decision. Of course, you did it to create another excuse for yourself to feel anger and sadness. Well, now you have a new reason to be angry, so be angry and be sad. I have to work and you know what? I don't plan to be angry and I don't plan to be sad. I won't be your accomplice in this. You're on your own," you said and hung up.

I threw my phone on the bed and took a deep breath. I couldn't stop thinking about my mother and how we parted. I felt guilty but I didn't know how to call her and apologize. I went into the guest bedroom so that I could smell her vanilla scent on the sheets. The room was completely empty and the bed was neatly made. I immediately recognized the way only my mother could make a bed. She had left a present behind for me, with a small note beside it. I started crying as I sat down on the bed. I stroked the bedding, hugged the pillow, and broke down.

"Mom, Mom, I'm sorry," I whispered softly into the pillow. "I'm so sorry, I love you, please don't be angry at me, I didn't mean it, I love you," I was shaking all over. I picked up the note and forced myself to read it.

"My Margot, I love you endlessly. That will never change. I'm sorry I failed to give you this gift in person. I want you to be happy. We all try every day and there is hope for each one of us. Never forget that. I'm sure your path is long and bright, and that countless flowers grow along it. You can do it, you deserve it. One day all things will fall into place because I know you will find your peace, and it will reveal to you how much you should be grateful for everything. Happy Birthday. Yours, Mom," she wrote. I felt deep pain reading her words.

The note opened a hole in me that was full of repentance. Nothing in my life had to be this way and I don't know why everything has always turned out like this.

I picked up the gift, and as I unwrapped it I remembered how much attention my mother always paid to details. When I was little and I went to my friends' birthday parties, I never had expensive or luxurious gifts, but my present was always the most beautifully wrapped. My mother taught me that small things are very important. Underneath the wrapping I found a box with a lid. I opened it and took out a beautiful dark blue blanket, which I immediately knew my mother had knitted for me. She hadn't knitted in a long time, but it used to be her great passion. I remember her knitting all the time when I was a child. I took the blanket in my hands and stretched it out over the bed. In the middle of the blanket, in small white letters, she knitted the word 'hope'. I curled up on the blanket and started kissing it, hugging it, wanting to feel my mother. I could feel all the love she made the blanket with. I could feel the dedication, I could feel the attention she invested in it. It was the most beautiful gift I had ever received.

I had to calm my nerves and I thought I should get out of the house as soon as possible. I thought I could go to Les Restos du Cœur and talk about my ideas for collaboration with the the Barcelona Women's Network. I wasn't prepared at all, I hadn't made a plan, nor had I started the process as agreed with Adrienne and Danielle, but I knew that once I got there we could get the ball rolling.

I left the room and shouted at Michaela that I was going out.

"Don't change the bedding in the guestbedroom," I instructed her.

I wanted her to leave that room the way it was so that I could keep my mother there for as long as possible. I left the note on my dresser drawer and the blanket over my bed, thrown across my pillow. I hurried out of the house, taking the subway to get there faster. Along the way I didn't know what excuse I would give to explain why I hadn't prepared anything for the project with the theBarcelona Women's Network,or why the previous day I failed to even call Danielle to tell her that I had guests and that I would come to the office at Les Restos du Cœur as soon as I could. I didn't want to lie.

I arrived at Les Restos du Cœur and took a deep breath. I walked down the halls confidently, but I was scared. I was afraid that the guilt I felt would be visible on my face. When a person is guilty, he or she thinks that everyone knows about it. I have been guilty for years, and maybe I have been guilty all my life.

I entered Danielle's office and Adrienne was there. They were working and jotting things down on a notepad.

"Margot, how are you? We thought you wouldn't come in today," said Adrienne, and Danielle just looked at me.

"I'm here, of course. I'm a little late, but here I am," I smiled, not knowing what else to say.

"That's the most important thing. Do you want coffee while we talk about the project with the Barcelona Women's Network?"

I was silent.

"Margot?"

"Yes, sure," I said, "I'm sorry, today is not my day."

"No problem. I'm going to get coffee. Danielle, coffee for you?"

She turned to Danielle and Danielle nodded.

After Adrienne left, I was quiet.

"Margot, what's going on? Are you falling apart again?" Danielle asked, and then she got up and came over to me.

124

"Yes," I replied, barely audible.

"It started well, then you underestimated your dark side thinking it was gone, and it grabbed you with its claws again. Am I right?"

She said it as if she had been with me all weekend and knew everything that had happened.

"Most likely," I said.

"Margot, there are diseases that come and go, and there are those that are part of us forever. We live with them and we can even become better people because of them, but that doesn't mean we should underestimate them and give them back their power, hoping that this time they won't try to kill us. For example, a recovering alcoholic turns into a person who once had a problem with alcohol, but that doesn't mean that the problem is permanently resolved. That's why it's very important to live your whole life properly, without giving power to your diseases. Do you know what an illusion is? It's an illusion when the same alcoholic after two years of abstinence thinks he can drink a few glasses from time to time because he no longer has a problem with alcohol, and can drink only when he wants to. And? Less than two months have passed - that person starts drinking again every day, and in the morning instead of coffee, he or she wakes up to something stronger," said Danielle and sat down again.

"You?"

"No, not me - my brother, he's passed away now. He chose to die. He gave strength to his disease and it killed him. He was young, smart, and as deep as the ocean. Unfortunately, he didn't understand life and he couldn't withstand the moments between the big waves," she sighed.

"Danielle, I'm so sorry. It must have been difficult for everyone. You hide it so well. I would tell people straight away if it was me, it would be my first conversation with someone," my voice trembled.

"It was difficult, it is still difficult. That's life. If you don't understand it, in time it can kill you early."

"I couldn't find the coffee, I thought we ran out and I was about to go shopping when I saw that we had moved it. I'm sorry I kept you waiting for so long," Adrienne said as she entered, handing us each a cup.

"Thank you," I said.

"You're welcome. Margot, please don't stand, it makes me feel superior and I don't want to feel that way. Sit, please sit," she showed me the chair with her hand, and I immediately took a seat, drinking my coffee.

"Okay, where are we now? Margot, did you think more about that idea? Did you manage to talk to the organization in Barcelona?"

"No, I didn't do anything about it and I apologize. I had a difficult weekend, I had guests and some unexpected things happened. I'll do it as soon as I can," I was ashamed of myself.

"Okay, I hope everything is fine now," she gave me a worried look.

"I hope so too," I said.

"Margot, this is a charitable organization and people who help come here because they want to, not because they have to. I don't want you coming here thinking anything is an obligation on you, it must be a pleasure. Of course there are responsibilities, but these are responsibilities that you don't experience as a hardship. If you feel burdened or maybe feel that you don't have enough time, I'll fully understand," she said, and I was surprised by her words.

"No no. It's quite the opposite of how I feel. Coming here has given light to my darkness, and after a long time I feel as if I'm in the right place. I found incredible happiness doing this work and I really don't want to stop. I'm sorry, but there are still parts of me that I need to work on. I'm sure of one thing, I know I never want to take a step back and be content with standing still. I want to go forward, to create, to discover, to help, to find out. That's why I'm here. Really. Believe me, my desire is huge,

I hope that my strength will be just as great," I said.

"Margot, I completely understand you. I don't doubt you and I don't want you to doubt yourself either. I want you to be safe, to have a good time here, and to feel comfortable," she smiled.

"It will be good," Danielle added, showing me support with the look in her eyes.

"Okay, then I'll leave you to start work, Danielle will tell you if you need to do anything else. I have some responsibilities, but tomorrow I want to see you again and talk about progress. Okay?"

She got up to leave then turned around suddenly and said, "Margot?"

"Yes?" I looked at her scared.

"I've been thinking about your idea all weekend. Brilliant idea, I thought," she smiled and left.

I felt relieved. I looked at Danielle, then smiled and said, "I have to start working right away."

"Great. Here is your computer and here is the phone, I'll go to the other room - if someone comes for an examination, I'll have to disturb you, but otherwise you can continue working here without interruption. There aren't many people today," she said.

"Danielle, thank you," I replied.

"Start working, don't thank me," she smiled and went out, closing the door. Not knowing where to start, I found the contact number for the Barcelona Women's Network online and called it. While the phone rang, I thought about how I would present my idea. I carefully chose each word I would use.

"Yes, Barcelona Women's Network, how can we assist you?" I heard a voice say. It was a polite female voice.

"Yes, I am calling from Les Restos du Cœur, we're a charitable organization based in Paris," I began, and after polite introductions, I explained why I was reaching out to them. I said I had an idea for possible collaboration between the two organizations, theirs, and Les Restos du Cœur.

"That sounds interesting," the lady said after I explained my thoughts. She told me her name was Miriam, and that she was one of the founding directors of the team in Barcelona. "I like the sound of the idea," she said, and that gave me more courage to speak.

I told her that among other things, Les Resto du Coeur has a department dedicated to giving support to parents with babies ranging in age from newborns to twelve months old, and that the organization helps young parents and parents who don't have enough support, by supplying them with necessary baby products, paediatric advice, and examinations.

"Through our support, we help parents, especially mothers, to cope with the demands of having a new baby, especially parents going through a particularly difficult period."

"That sounds really wonderful."

"Yes, we have a whole department here that's fully committed to promoting this agenda. Given that you offer support to women, I thought that such an initiative would benefit you. It gives the concept of supporting motherhood for struggling mothers a broader geographic reach and I hope that it can expand into even more regions through collaborations such as the one that I'm suggesting to you now. Eventually, we'd like this kind of support to exist globally, as it's an important need that's not being adequately addressed."

"I really love the idea," she said, "this kind of help is in short supply, even here in Barcelona. Tell me, how do you think we can proceed to realize this?"

"We should start with a workshop here at our offices in Paris. We are eager to facilitate the exchange of information, particularly regarding the operational management systems we have in place. Once you understand this concept in more detail, you could develop it in Barcelona too, with our support."

"I like it, but it will take money to execute, am I right? Even the workshop alone will require travel and funding for

tickets, and a stay in Paris for various members of our g
It may not be big money, but for us at the moment, every l
is important. I'm going to be honest with you, we, like most
charitable organizations, are funded by public funds and some
private donors. But in recent years the situation has been really
difficult. We had a lot of ideas and big projects that remained
unrealized because of financial constraints. Currently, we
operate with a very small budget. I really can't see how we
would implement this," she explained.

"I understand," I sighed.

"It's a great idea, and such a thing would be incredibly
useful here. At the end of the day, what kind of women's charity
organization are we if we don't support and help mothers?
Unfortunately, the world isn't fair, dear Margot, money is
thrown at some causes, while others are ignored."

"That's true yes," I said in a dejected voice.

"I'm glad we talked to each other, maybe we can put this on
the timeline for the future."

"The pleasure is mine, thank you very much for the time,"
I said.

We greeted each other and hung up. I slouched over the
desk where I sat, stung by her words. It was a pity. I knew it
meant my idea was off, and that disappointed me.

"What happened?" Danielle asked, stepping into the office.
I looked up.

"I was talking to a woman who is part of the founding team
at the Barcelona Women's Network, Miriam she said her name
was. I told her the idea and she really liked it. Unfortunately,
she explained to me that their budget has been very limited
lately, and that many important projects have remained
unrealized. They just don't have the means to come to Paris for
the workshop, let alone for something bigger."

"That's a pity," said Danielle.

"She said there are so many essential causes with no

financial support. She also said that they are not a real women's organization if they don't support mothers, but you need a budget, and they don't have one big enough for this right now."

"I'm sorry Margot, I know you believed in this idea," she came up to me and hugged me.

"I still believe in it," I said.

"Hope is the ground on which you stand, without it there is only a hole."

"Yes," I sighed.

"Why don't you go home now, we can manage here this afternoon."

"You're sure?"

"Yes, go home and rest. Rest your soul. Then, come back tomorrow. Tomorrow is a new day," she held my hand.

"Okay, see you tomorrow Danielle. We'll talk to Adrienne tomorrow too," I said.

"No problem, go and rest," she smiled.

I left Les Restos du Cœur and headed home. On the subway I couldn't stop thinking about the Barcelona Women's Network and our conversation. As I thought about it, I began to travel to new horizons and I literally felt like I was coming out of my safe shell and slowly smelling the real scent of the world. If there is peace within our four walls, it doesn't mean there is no war outside of it, and that it's not our responsibility to help, I thought.

Arriving home with no desire for anything, I decided to confront reality and start making small differences. Although I couldn't change the world for the better, I could always change myself. Over the years, frustrated within the bounds of society, I sat idly by, thinking I had the right to do so.

I was wrong. Who am I to be disappointed by the world? What have I done for the world to expect anything in return? My mother's words rang through my mind.

At home I decided to go buy some flowers, and Michaela

was surprised to see me leaving right after I came in.

"I want to buy blue irises and plant them in our garden," I said. "You know I love blue irises. I've long wanted to plant some in our garden, but I don't know why I never did. Really Michaela, why did I never do that? What was stopping me, when in fact nothing was stopping me?"

"Margot, don't obsess over past failings. The important thing is that you're planting irises today. That's the only thing that matters now," smiled Michaela.

"You're right," I smiled and rushed out.

The flowershop near our house was closed because it was Tuesday, so I went somewhere else. I was in a hurry, as if someone was chasing me. I felt an incredible need to act. I was tired of my excuses.

I was bored of myself Arthur, do you believe that? I couldn't do it anymore. Something had to change forever, me, for example.

In the flowershop I chose the most beautiful blue irises. When I saw them it was as if they saw me. I knew immediately that they were mine. I picked them up and hurried home. I felt a kind of special joy and couldn't wait to plant them in our garden.

When I came home Michaela was ready to leave. We exchanged two, three words, and I went straight to the garden to plant them. Irises need at least six hours of sunlight a day, and our garden is fully exposed to the sun. I scooped out some soil, making holes in the dirt. For irises the hole should not be too deep. On the other hand, the hole I fell into was incredibly deep. I wasn't about to make the same mistake with my beautiful blue irises.

On my knees in the garden I felt completely carefree. I planted the flowers, covered them well with earth and then watered them. "Welcome home," I said, standing up.

I took a shower to wash away the grime, to wash away all of my guilt. I felt free. It was too early to fall asleep but I was tired. I didn't know when you'd get home so I picked up a new sheet of paper and started writing. When I heard you coming in, I hid the sheet of paper.

You came into the bedroom and asked, "Margot, what are you doing?"

"Nothing, I'm just resting," I said.

"How was your day?"

"Okay, better than yesterday."

"That's good."

"I planted some blue irises in our garden."

"What made you decide to do that?"

"Because I've always wanted to do it and today I just thought, well, nothing was stopping me," I sighed.

"You're right about that."

"There aren't many, only a few, but that counts as something too."

"My dear Margot, a few blue irises make an entire garden," you nodded. "I'll watch TV downstairs. I'm going to sleep there," you paused and then you said, "we're still going to Antibes on Thursday?"

"The day after tomorrow, I know. Yes."

"Good night Arthur."

You went out and closed the door.

I continued writing when you were gone. As I'm writing this, emotions come out of me like never before. I felt good when I saw you.

Yours,
    Margot

P.S. Thank you for believing that a few irises make an entire garden.

CHAPTER SIXTEEN

August 21, 2019

My dear Arthur,

Themorning before our trip to Antibes you were asleep downstairs in the living room, wrapped in a blanket with one foot almost touching the ground. I bent over you to cover you with the blanket and you woke up immediately.

"Margot, what time is it?"

"Five twenty," I smiled at you. "It's early, get some more sleep."

"And why are you awake?"

"I'm not tired. I'm going to water the irises. Sleep, then I'll make you some coffee later," I said and went into the garden. You turned to the other side and fell asleep again. I thought you looked like you were exhausted.

In the garden I took a deep breath. It was tranquil out there and I reached out to touch my blue irises and started talking to them. My father always told me that flowers should be talked to, because like humans, they want attention.

"Good morning my blue beauties, how are you today?I hope you feel good here. I'm very happy that you're part of our garden and I hope that one day this whole space will be full of you. I adore you so much." I started watering them. "I want you to be happy here. I'm not an example to you, to be honest. I may not know what happiness is, but I know what misfortune is, and I can tell you that there's no place for both in one place. One who is happy will always choose happiness. A happy person won't use even the greatest misfortune as an excuse to be unhappy. It's a matter of choice. I wish for each of you to be happy here, my beautiful irises," I told them.

"Beautifully said," I heard your voice and turned around, you were standing behind me with a soft smile on your lips. "And you, Margot?"

You approached me.

"What about me?"

"Can you be happy here?"

You came very close to me, placing your hands on my shoulders, causing me to tremble.

"I don't know," I replied.

"I think you can. It's true that it's a matter of choice," you said, and completely unexpectedly you kissed me. I didn't anticipate that. Every bit of me was nervous but it felt right. I didn't fight you, I gave in and put my arms around your neck. We kissed like teenagers in love, like kissing was a very important thing. Quite close to my blue irises, a small miracle happened.

After pulling your lips away from mine, you said in a daze, "I'm going to get ready for work. You can get some packing done for our trip tomorrow."

"I think I should," I said, like I was floating.

"Have a great day," you said going back into the house, and I stood in the garden feeling incredibly different, but good.

I stayed in our garden for another hour and enjoyed every moment of it. As the sun kept on rising, my blue irises seemed so happy, as if they were smiling toward the sunshine. When I went back into the house you had already left for work. Just like my irises, I was smiling like never before. I went up to the bedroom and started preparing for the trip. My plan was to go to Les Restos du Cœur, then to the shops to buy some things for our trip to Antibes, and finally to come home again to get ready.

In the shower I sang aloud to a song by Edith, the lyrics went something like, "in love there must be tears, in love it is necessary to give something!" I had always liked the song, but now I really understood what it meant. I continued to sing the words as I got ready, and was still singing it when I came downstairs.

"What a mood we have today," Michaela greeted me.

"That's right, I have to admit," I smiled,"I don't know why, but it is a good mood."

"A smile doesn't need an explanation, it's important to have it that's all."

"I have to go to Les Restos du Cœur and then I have to do some last minute shopping. We're going to Antibes for my birthday, and to get a little rest," I said.

"My dear Margot, I really hope this trip revitalizes you and brings you peace of mind," she said.

"Peace? Yes, I want that too. I've always wanted just a little peace, but I suppose I'm also the one making my own path difficult," I sighed.

"Everything will be fine, have a great trip," she added.

"You too, dear," I said and went out. I took the car because I was planning to go shopping. As I drove to Les Restos du Cœur, I began to think about the organization from Barcelona and how that idea hadn't materialized. I really believed in that project and I took the disappointment personally. The world really arranges its priorities unfairly, the idea that so many important projects fail to see the light of day, causing so many people not to get the help they need, troubled me.

Adrienne greeted me at the entrance of Les Restos du Cœur's office. She told me that I looked different and I wondered if it was just a general statement or if she could really notice that I was happier.

"Yes," she said, "something's different, you're glowing."

I blushed.

"Let's go inside, Danielle is there," Adrienne suggested. We walked in together as she began discussing the Barcelona project. "I asked Danielle about your idea this morning, and she told me what happened. Don't be disappointed, that's how it goes sometimes."

"It's hard for me to accept, I took it very personally," I said.

"That means you have a spirit and a heart, so don't feel silly for being affected."

"Yes?"

"Yes. I've been doing this for a long time, and over the years I've come to learn that people who create with their heart and soul always find their way. Remember, the universe loves such people and helps them," she smiled.

"Danielle, Margot is here," she said, knocking on the door.

"Come in," Danielle said, and my gaze fixed on the large crowd in the back room.

"There are a lot of people here today," I said.

"Yes, today is one of those days," Adrienne replied.

"Sit down Margot, sit down," Adrienne said, and I sat down.

"Margot, I don't want you to be disappointed, your idea is wonderful, we all think so. We'll see what happens. Keep believing," Adrienne encouraged me.

"That's right, Margot knows that hope is the basis of everything. I'm also sure she knows that the problem isn't with her idea, but with society, with the world, to be more specific."

"With the world," I repeated, though I was completely preoccupied. My thoughts were with the crowd.

"Margot, are you okay?" Adrienne asked.

"I'm fine. Do you know what? We may not be able to change the world, but we can change this situation here. I want to help, I don't want to get stuck on what hasn't succeeded," I said, and Adrienne and Danielle were impressed by that.

"Told you so. I told you that you just have to push her a little bit, and she'd be flying by herself," Danielle said to Adrienne, and we all laughed. "Come on, Margot, let's go over there," Danielle said, getting up.

"See you later," Adrienne greeted us and left.

"You grow every day," Danielle said, and handed me a piece

of paper which read: *'Here is your list.'*

"It's very important to find out who needs what and to speak to everyone openly from the heart. If it happens that we don't have what someone needs, it's important that you write it down so that we know."

"Okay, where do I start?" I looked around.

"At the beginning dear, always at the beginning," she smiled and left me alone. I knew that I would only learn something new that way. I was starting from scratch, and I didn't know where to find the beginning. The other volunteers and staff were already scattered throughout the room, it seemed a bit chaotic. There were too many people, mothers with crying babies, pregnant women, men and women arguing loudly, and there were some quiet women at the back of the room, not saying a word to anyone. I had to make a start.

I approached a pregnant woman who looked very scared and said, "Hello, I'm Margot, I work here as a volunteer. How can I help you?"

"Hello, I'm Anna," she said, looking at me with tears in her eyes.

"Anna, how can I help you? I see you're pregnant, congratulations," I said.

"Yes, I'm pregnant. Six months. You know what, I really don't know what I'm doing here. Until the other day I had a partner who was looking forward to the child we're having together. We're not married but we were in love, and for me that's everything. I lost my job when he told me to come and help him at the souvenir shop where he works. He said he needed me there and that it would be our family business. I tried to work there with him and keep my job at the hotel as well, because it was a secure job, but between trying to keep both jobs and my pregnancy as well - I couldn't keep up. Everything changed. He broke up with me and said he wasn't ready to be a father. I lost my job and the bills piled up. I have no idea how I'm going to afford everything I need, and my debts keep growing. I'm not lazy, I'll find a job again, but that's where I need your help. I want to know if you can really help me with the baby in the beginning? Any support will mean a lot to me. I'm completely alone. I don't have a family. I have nothing. I have nowhere to leave the child while I'm at work and I don't know anyone who can even give my baby toys or nappies. We're all alone," she began to cry, and I hugged her. "I want to give birth to this baby, I won't give up my baby, I want to keep him," she continued, "I just need a little help to get on my feet," she trembled.

"Anna, I completely understand, I really sympathize with your situation. Believe me, you're in the right place. We exist to help people like you. Your story's touched my heart and we are an organization that works from the heart, for the hearts of all others. We'll do everything we can," I hugged her once more.

"Thank you," she smiled, "who knew that this would be my life," she sighed, and immense sympathy for her stirred in me.

"Your life can change, you can make it change," I encouraged her.

"Do you believe that?"

"I do," I smiled at her, "you know what? I'm going to talk to our paediatrician to see what we can do for you. I'll be back in a minute. She's amazing, you'll see," I touched her shoulder and started looking for Danielle. I spotted her and went over to get her so that she could speak to Anna.

After I introduced them, Danielle said, "I want to tell you that you're very brave and we'll do everything we can to help you."

"Really?"

She cried and through her tears she said, "Thank you so much."

"Yes. Don't worry. We're here to support you in every way we can."

"Beginnings are always difficult, but you will get through

this," Danielle comforted her.

"Thank you," she trembled.

"Margot told me you're in the sixth month of your pregnancy, is that right?"

"Yes, that's right," Anna confirmed.

"Great. Now the most important thing is to take care of your health, because your health is important for the little baby you're going to bring into the world," and as Danielle said that, Anna stroked her pregnant stomach.

"Boy or girl?"

"Boy," she said answering me, her eyes lighting up. "He's a boy, but I'll raise him to be a good man," she joked.

"I have no doubt," I said.

"Ok. If you need any help while you're pregnant, or someone to talk to, or a medical examination, whatever, feel free to ask me," Danielle handed her a card.

"Thank you, I'm really speechless," she didn't stop thanking us.

After completing a few more tasks I was ready to leave and went into Danielle's office to say goodbye.

"You were great today. This is how it's done. People need support, courage and ... "

"And hope," I added.

"And hope. You know that without hope, there's nothing," she smiled.

"I'm leaving for Antibes tomorrow. I'll be there until Sunday," I said, a little self-conscious.

"Yes? Very nice," she looked at me with a look that said everything.

"Yes. It's my birthday on Sunday so we're going to celebrate. His idea," I explained.

"I've noticed that you find it awkward to talk about happiness. You shouldn't. If you had bad news, you'd talk to me about it with no qualms, but happiness is harder to talk about. It's strange, you feel like something's wrong with you, don't you?"

She tapped the desk with her pen.

"Something like that," I was embarrassed.

"Let all the darkness go, I say. Don't you dare hold onto it or miss it when it leaves. It isn't real, you know."

"I know," I went up to her and hugged her tightly.

"You give me light, too," I said, "see you on Monday."

"See you, my dear," she sent me off with a smile.

After leaving Les Restos du Cœur I went to the shops. I felt like I needed a lot of things, but maybe I was just nervous.

I filled my shopping basket, and as I ran around grabbing items I needed for the trip, I started to feel ill. My hands were shaky, and I got lost in the shopping aisles. A sense of panic gripped me and I tried to fight, but I felt uncertain. I was determined not to ruin our trip, and as long as the anxiety of going didn't ruin me first, I knew Antibes was a good idea.

When I got home I was glad to find that no one was there, because I wanted to get ready for the trip, alone. The morning kiss never left my mind, Arthur, but I didn't want to think about what it meant. I went up to the bedroom and put on some music - an upbeat song that I knew the words to came on the radio and I started singing along to it. As I moved around the room doing chores, I started dancing to the beat. I took out a big suitcase that I hadn't used for a long time, and next to it I saw the bag which, just two weeks ago, I had planned to throw a few items of clothing into and walk out the front door, leaving you forever, Arthur. Unanswered questions came over me like a cloud, but I didn't have the strength to play this game. Ah, how tired I am of myself, I thought.

I packed all my toiletries and essentials, and the few things I bought at the shops, but I really couldn't decide which clothes to take. I looked through my cupboard and found my favorite bathing suit, which we happened to have bought in Antibes. I remembered that I had tried it on some time ago and I couldn't look at myself in the mirror when I did. I remembered how neglected and unattractive I thought I looked, I remember thinking that such a bathing suit shouldn't be worn by someone like me. Recalling how I felt, I pondered if I should take the bathing suit with me. I didn't want to try it on again, I just wanted to believe what I had thought then wasn't true. I folded it up and threw it into the suitcase.

"You're coming with me," I said aloud, feeling like it was a victory. Finally, I packed my favorite picture, one of my father and I, and I said to myself, "Nowhere without you."

After a few hours I was absolutely ready. My suitcase for Antibes was packed.

I heard your voice coming from downstairs, "Margot, I'm home!"

You came into the bedroom and saw me sitting on the bed, my suitcase leaning against the wardrobe.

"And a hat?"

"I completely forgot!"

I remembered the events that took place the day I went hat shopping with my mother. I hung my head.

"What is it now?"

"Nothing, I'm thinking about my mother, that time she was here, we wanted to buy the same hats but we had an argument and I left the mall," I said with my head down.

You came to sit next to me and asked, "Ok, that's all finished now. Speaking of your mother, did you call her?"

"No, she didn't call me either," I said.

"You should call her," you looked at me.

"I don't know, I really don't know."

"Or write her a letter," you said.

I turned pale.

"I beg your pardon?"

"I said, write her a letter, if you can't call her, send her an email. I know your mother has an email address. Some people find writing easier," you smiled at me and got up again.

The comment about writing bothered me. I thought to myself, you know nothing Arthur. You suggest I write a letter or an email because in your business world that's how people communicate. But you don't know that I'm the woman who writes letters to her husband every night and doesn't give them to him. I put my thoughts on paper because I can't tell you how I feel, so I resort to talking to myself. You aren't right Arthur, writing isn't easy at all, if you're looking for the truth.

"You look tired, rest a bit. I'll go downstairs to watch some TV," you said.

"Aren't you tired too?" I asked.

"I will be in an hour or so, and then I'll come here to lie down. Can I?" You looked at me.

"Yes," I said.

"Good night," you smiled, closing the door.

I didn't wait a minute. I started writing. There was silence in the room but my sighs could be heard. Deep, loving sighs, full of fresh air.

Yours,

Margot

P.S. Maybe I will listen to you. I think one day I will write a letter to my mother and tell her everything.

CHAPTER SEVENTEEN

August 22, 2019

My dear Arthur,

This morning we woke up in the same bed and at the same time. Waking up, I looked into your deep eyes, staring at me. You smiled and I smiled too. It didn't feel strange to see you next to me. I didn't notice what time you came to bed last night because I was fast asleep. I slept well for the first time in a while.It meant a lot when you asked if you could lie next to me.I thought it was the perfect time for us to try and reconnect. You were an absolute gentleman and you respected my space. I don't know how, but I guess you just knew I wasn't ready for anything more than just sharing a bed, not yet.

After we got up, I made us coffee while you took a shower. We drank the coffee together in silence, but I could feel we were communicating without talking. I took a shower straight after you and felt an excitement run through my entire body as the drops of water touched my skin, signalling to me that I was truly ready for our trip together.

We went to Antibes with your car, as we usually do. Although the trip isn't short, you always said it was best to drive there.

"Eight hours in the car. Will we endure?"

I smiled as you drove.

"We'll cope with this," you said, and pulled a CD out of the compartment in the car door. I saw that you had the same CD that I have, the one by Edith Piaf - I was surprised.

"I didn't know you had one of those too, it's my favorite."

"One would be enough if we listened to it together," you

smiled and handed it to me.

You asked me to put on the sont, "I Do Not Regret Anything."

"I was listening to that recently in my car," I said, popping in the CD.

"And?"

"And what?" I asked as the song came on and I turned the volume up.

"And? Do you regret anything?"

You raised your voice over the music.

"I don't regret anything at all. I'm ready for a change and although life will never be as it was before, it doesn't mean that it won't be beautiful," I said loudly.

"Did you come up with that now?"

I knew you were just teasing me. "No, this is from the other day," I smiled, and we started laughing together. I realized that I used to get angry at you for such comments, because I thought you didn't take me seriously, but now I see there's nothing wrong with laughing at yourself sometimes. It doesn't mean you don't respect me, Arthur.

While listening to Edith, I fell asleep. I don't know how I dozed off so easily. Maybe it happened because I felt safe. Usually when we traveled, I would complain about everything. I was constantly irritated by this or that - either you were driving too fast, or the road seemed too long, or the music was too loud for me, or I couldn't stand the noise - but the impossible happened now. You played loud music and I fell asleep.

When I woke up, I didn't know what time it was or where we were.

"Arthur, where are we?" I asked.

"Almost in Antibes. We'll be there in twenty minutes," you said.

"You mean to tell me I slept that long?"

I looked at you in astonishment.

"Yes, you slept for seven hours, you were awake for only the first hour of our trip and then you disappeared," you smiled.

"And you?"

"I was driving, I stopped several times," you said.

"Arthur, I'm sorry, I don't know how I could've slept for so long. I thought I wasn't tired, I don't understand."

"Your body wasn't tired, but your soul was. The drive relaxed you. Margot, this was the best trip I've ever had with you. There is nothing wrong with relaxing and sleeping. We listened to some music and then you fell asleep. That's perfectly normal. It means you're feeling calm, you're not restless or anxious," you said with incredible peace in your voice.

"I think so too. I've never been able to do that before."

"I know, but you said it yourself - you're ready for a change, aren't you?"

"Yes. What are we going to do when we arrive? And what time is it? We'll be there in twenty minutes, so it'll be six o'clock," I began with my questions.

"Margot, we're on vacation for the next five days. Can we agree on something?"

"Yes, what."

"No plans, no rules, no schedule. There are only moments and everything depends on them. Agreed?"

"You know it's not easy for me, but I promise I'll try," I smiled.

"And I promise to help you," you held out your right hand, "so we have a deal?"

"We have an agreement," I said.

"I can't hear you, maybe a little louder? Do we have an agreement?!"

"We have an agreement!"

I shouted and we both started laughing out loud.

In a short time we arrived at the villa in Antibes.

"I've forgotten how beautiful it is," I said, entering.

The furniture was mostly in natural tones and looked timeless. I was reminded of how much fun we used to have here. When you first brought me to Antibes after we got married, this place was our honeymoon spot. You were always so emotional when speaking about the villa because it had been in your family for a long time and your father used to love it.

"Yes, it really is beautiful," you said, carrying the suitcases.

"And the yard, look how gorgeous the yard is. And the pool, I love tanning by the pool," I said.

"Yes, I arranged for it to be maintained from time to time," you explained.

"Really? I feel like you think of everything."

"No, that's your job. I don't think of everything, I just know when to act."

"You know what I remembered? How much we played pétanque here in the yard? Do you recall how much better I was than you?"

I started to enjoy teasing you.

"I remember we played, but I don't remember you being better than me. It's not a big deal, I'll give you a chance to prove yourself," you said, standing in front of me.

"Oh, really? When?"

"Now, at this moment," you said.

"Now?"

"Yes, now. I'm sure the metal boules and the cochonnet are in the basement somewhere, I'm going to look for them," you said and headed for the basement.

"Arthur, we've just arrived, we haven't even unpacked."

"Margot, we said no plans, no schedule, and no rules. There are only moments," you reminded me, and the smile on my face came back.

We went out into the villa's yard and started playing.

"Why should you be first?" I said. "We need to spin a coin, that's the rules."

"Never forget the rules! You're right, you're right. I just wanted to see if you were focused," you teased, and stroked my face. "Come on, throw this coin," you handed it to me, "if it's heads, then you're first. If it's tails, then the better one is first, that is, me," you did not stop being playful.

"Let's see," I tossed the coin and it fell to the ground and landed on heads.

"Beginner's luck."

"Me, a beginner? You must be confused. So, I'm first. Can I start?" I stood proudly.

"Start, feel free," you said.

We played and had a great time, laughing and teasing each other. I felt like I was playing with my best friend. I could hardly believe it was us.

"You know I'm a winner right now, don't you?" I said somewhere in the middle of the game.

"Now I'm the winner," you said, swooping in to kiss me, then you retreated, as if we were children.

We played, forgetting about the time and we didn't stop laughing.

"It's over, it's over!" I shouted at the end of the game. "I beat you, I beat you!" I was so happy.

"You were lucky, nothing else."

"I want you to say out loud that I'm the winner."

"No chance," you refused.

"I want you to say out loud that I'm the winner!"

"No chance!"

"I want you to say it!"

You embraced me and lifted me up in your arms, carrying me inside the villa. We fell onto the living room floor and you kissed me passionately. Our clothes fell all around us, and when you touched me I felt like volcano. For the first time in a long time we made love. I don't remember great details because I was lost in the moment. I didn't try to understand anything, I completely surrendered to the feelings that you evoked in me. It was better than our first time, it was more than I imagined possible. It wasn't just about physical connection.

It was about merging two distant souls who had wandered in opposite directions for too long, and were now brought back together, where they belonged.

While I'm writing this letter, you're taking a shower and I'm sitting in the yard. It's wonderful outside. My words in these letters are less serious to me now because I feel like I'm starting to live again. The long conversations I had with you through writing these brought me to this point. I know the magic didn't happen today. What happened today was the result of self-work, honesty, and facing my pain.

Yours,

    Margot

P.S. Arthur, you know what? Any game can be fun if we really know how to have fun. Also, any game can destroy you while playing it, if you play with the intention of destruction.

CHAPTER EIGHTEEN

August 23, 2019

My dear Arthur,

This morning we woke up at the same time and in the same bed again, but this time we spooned and cuddled.

"Good morning," I said, sweetly.

"Good morning," you replied, and gently touched my forehead with your hand, "you have a pimple on your forehead."

"Yes? It will pass," I smiled.

"You used to get angry when I told you things like that, "you said, kissing me.

"Because you never complimented me. You never told me I was beautiful."

"I didn't tell you because I thought, and I still think, that a beautiful and confident woman should know she's beautiful and not wait for someone else to tell her. And by the way, I've always said that I have the most beautiful wife, a ginger beauty with deep green eyes."

"Really?"

"Are you surprised, did you doubt it?"

You kissed me again.

"It seems I doubted myself," I sighed.

"Don't worry about that now. Let's go to the beach and grab a bite to eat," you suggested.

"The beach? You don't want to be at the pool here?"

"I want to be around people a little bit," you said, getting out of bed.

"Why?"

"Because I want you to be comfortable around people, strangers I mean, and not just be comfortable around me. I want you to be confident like the Margot I first fell in love with, even when there's a crowd and there's a lot of noise, and we can barely exchange two words. You must be comfortable even when it's uncomfortable. It'll help you get out of your comfort zone," you smiled.

"Arthur, you surprise me. I never knew that ... "

And before I could continue you interrupted me to finish my sentence, "Knew what? That I know you so well?"

"Stop it!" I shouted and threw my pillow at you playfully.

"You're dead now!"

You got on the bed and started tickling me, covering me with the other pillow. We laughed without end. It was amazing and we stayed in bed doing nothing for at least another two hours, just enjoying being with each other. We talked very little, the silence was enough for us. I forgot about time and every other worry slipped away.

"If we don't go out now, I think we'll stay here all day," you smiled.

"We don't have rules?" I reminded you.

"Oh, that's right, but let's go to the beach, okay?"

You kissed me.

"Maybe," I smiled.

"You get ready, I need to go downstairs for five minutes to check something," you said and left the room.

I got up to take a shower and felt like I was another woman. I was finally getting to know myself. After I dried myself with the towel, I put on my bathing suit and checked my reflection in the mirror. I liked what I saw, and just then you came into the room.

"What a bathing suit, looks great on you," you said.

"Do you really like it?" I turned.

"Love it. We bought that here, didn't we? I always liked the way it looked on you," you said and went into the bathroom. I looked back at my reflection in the mirror and turned from side to side. Yes, I thought, I liked it too.

"Arthur?" I called, putting a hat on my head.

"Yes?"

You popped your head out of the bathroom door.

"Remember I used to run regularly?"

"Yes, I remember," you said, coming toward me.

"And then I stopped suddenly. Running used to really calm me down."

"So, start running again."

"You think I could just pick up where I left off, that simple?"

"No, it's not simple at all. Do you know why?" You put your arms around me. "If you start running again, this beautiful body of yours will tighten even more and then you'll have no reason to complain about your physical appearance, and that's a problem for you. So no, it won't be simple at all, but the right path is never easy," you kissed me on my forehead.

"You're right, it's not easy," I sighed. "Arthur?"

"Yes?"

"Why couldn't we speak to each other this easily all that time? Why did we struggle so much?"

"I guess you stopped telling me things and I stopped asking after you. Nobody started first, we both got lost at the same time."

"You were lost too?" I looked at you.

"If we attract sorrow to our home and chase away happiness, our home will turn into a sad home. In a sad home Margot, there are only lost people," you sighed.

I put my fingers to your lips to silence you. I didn't want to talk about anything anymore. I looked in your eyes and kissed you, and the truth was clear. There were two injured people living together in our house, two lost people, and I foolishly thought I was the only one. I locked myself up with the walls I built around me. I didn't understand then that when something falls apart, everyone has the right to grieve. Did I really think the grief only belonged to me? Was I that selfish? Our grief is special, Arthur. We created it ourselves, but it gives me hope that just as we have managed to create sorrow, we can also create joy - and that happiness, will be very special.

"Which beach are we going to?" I asked you as we left the villa.

"Our beach," you smiled.

"Do we have a beach?"

"We, my dear - have everything. And how much we value what we have - I don't know," you sighed, and took me by the hand. I felt safe.

Going to the beach, my soul was calm. I didn't mind that it was too hot and that I could hardly breathe. My body was relaxed and I had no trembling or shaky hands because of anxiety. My mind didn't race at all and all my thoughts aligned to my physical peace.

"Where is this beach? Have we been there before?"

"No, this beach is new," you smiled. I knew that you were trying to get me out of my comfort zone, and I decided to let you.

"I love Antibes," you said.

"Me too."

"I love France," you said.

"Me too."

"I love life," you said, and immediately looked at me, smiling. "Will you repeat that after me?" You challenged me, and I lowered my eyes, stopping.

"I don't know if it's true."

"I know it is. I'm sure it's true."

"You think I love life? Do you really mean that? What if it's just a phase I'm going through, what if it changes?" I asked.

"Everything can change, but everything can be learned again. One can always learn new skills," you said.

"Skills? Do you think it's a skill to love life?" I looked at you.

"Yes, it's one of the most beautiful skills. Seemingly simple, but in fact incredibly difficult to learn."

"Incredibly hard to learn, that's right," I sighed.

"Do you know who told me that?" You smiled at me and I could have guessed.

"My mother?"

"Yes."

"I guess it sounds like her. You know what, Arthur, would you believe me if I tell you it was only a few days ago I realized how wise my mother is? I never thought that about her before."

"Do you want me to tell you some good news?" You held my face in your palms.

"Yes."

"The rudder of your life is in your hands," you kissed me. I smiled, not letting myself get stuck in thoughts of the past. All I can do is try to be better, I thought.

"Shall we go?" You took my hand and we walked on. I felt great.

When we arrived at the beach you started looking for an empty spot and spoke to one of the attendants there.

"Yes, we would like two beach reclining chairs as close to the water as possible," you explained, and I stepped forward, wanting to put my feet in the water. I held my hat with my hand and made small ripples in the waves washing over my feet. There were children playing on the sand, jumping, and running. The seaside was fun for them. On the other side I saw a couple kissing. The seaside was love to them, I thought. I looked at the water, at the small ripples I was making with my toes by splashing it around and realized that the life we live will always be a mirror of ourselves. There were so many walks, vacations, parties, and events I remembered as bad parts of my life, not thinking that perhaps I was the one who made them like that.

"Margot, are you okay? We have our beach chairs, come on," I heard your voice say.

"Yes, I'm fine. I was looking at the sea," I smiled.

"Let's go," you said and held out your hand.

We were lying in the sun with an incredibly pleasant silence. I used to get angry when it was quiet, thinking it was a sign that we had nothing to say to each other, but letting go of that, I experienced the pleasure of just being near you.

"Margot, are you asleep?"

"No, I'm enjoying the sun," I smiled.

"I want to ask you something. Do you think you would have been happy if everything was exactly the way you wanted it to be?" I took my hat off my face, opening my eyes.

"Probably not," I sighed.

"And now?"

"I'm struggling now. I struggle with myself every day, but I'm definitely getting better at this life thing. Dissatisfaction is a brazen disease that appears imperceptibly because you attract it to yourself," I said.

"Do you think it's a disease?"

"I think everything that hurts is a disease, only there are diseases that disappear, there are those that you die from, and those that you have to learn to live with."

"I agree," you stretched out on the beach recliner again.

"Are you hungry?"

"Yes, I'm hungry - how about you?"

"I'm hungry too. Let's order something. Should we get fish?" you suggested.

"Yes, sure," I handed you the menu that the attendant had given to me earlier. "You know what?"

"What?"

You looked at the menu.

"Imagine the following situation. Two people are living in the same house and not talking to each other because they think they speak different languages and they don't understand each other. Time passes and they don't speak at all. One day by accident, one of them can't find the remote control for the

TV and has no choice but to ask the other person, in his own language, if he knows where the remote control is. The other person replies in that language and it occurs to them that they understand each other very well. They continue talking and the conversation flows with ease. They concluded that the reason they thought they didn't understand each other was because they didn't even try," I said.

"An interesting situation? This is you and I?"

You looked at me as the attendant arrived and we ordered our meals.

"Yes, in a way - this is us," I said.

"I disagree."

"Why?"

"Because regardless of whether the two of them think they understand each other or not, the fact that they aren't trying to understand each other tells me that they don't understand themselves. The most important thing is to talk to yourself first, and only after that conversation can you be ready to talk to other people."

"Maybe," I smiled.

"I won't let you feel dissatisfied again. You have to understand that everything is as it should be."

"Yes, but I regret so many things and I'd like to go back and change them. I feel guilty, I feel ashamed, all of that," I lowered my head.

"It's okay. Repentance is a lesson, guilt is soul-searching, and shame is re-examination. All of these things are part of human growth. Dissatisfaction is a curse that leads nowhere," you said.

"Ok Arthur, have you and I ever talked like this? Even at the beginning - has it ever been with such depth and sincerity?"

"I don't think so, but as you said - maybe our happiness will be special. Our sadness was definitely special. We deserve this ending, what do you think?"

You winked at me and I threw myself into your arms, saying

nothing more.

"Let's have a club sandwich," I smiled.

"A club sandwich sounds just perfect."

After a long, wonderful day at the beach we returned to the villa. The sun made us tired and we wanted to go to bed. Like yesterday, you took a shower and I used the time to write. This time Arthur, I didn't just write because I needed to talk to myself or to you. This time I wrote because I wanted this beautiful day to happen to me all over again, even if only on paper.

Yours,

Margot

P.S. Writing this letter I realized how alive I felt today. I wasn't absent, lost, or carried away. I was present, aware, and liberated - and we? We were in love.

CHAPTER NINETEEN

August 24, 2019

My dear Arthur,

The day before my birthdayI felt absolutely no pressure. I had no special wishes because I don't believe there's anything I need. I woke up grateful for what I have, knowing if I continue to work on myself, life will take me in the right direction and along the way it will give me beautiful flowers, as my mother said. I am conscious of having all the joys I dreamed of. I can truthfully say I didn't feel dissatisfied before my birthday this year, for the first time in a long time. I don't imagine my life differently. Everything was as it should be and I was happy. I was slowly getting rid of vain longing and wandering in the world of sorrow.

The phone woke me up this morning while you were still asleep. Snug in your arms, I could barely force myself to answer. When I saw Danielle's number, I thought it might be important so I answered and asked if everything was ok. She said everything was fine, but she had to call me.

"You won't believe what happened," Danielle said over the phone.

"Tell me - what?"

I was impatient and curious.

"This morning that organization, you know the Barcelona Women's Network - they called."

My heart rate went up a little hearing that, and I asked Danielle to tell me more.

"Miriam phoned and said that after talking to you she shared the idea with her colleagues. Everyone loved the idea and so they decided to send out an email about it, highlighting the funds that would be required for implementation to all potential donors they have a long-standing relationship with. They do this with all the ideas they believe in strongly, just in case funding can be raised. She said they expected nothing, but then yesterday someone contacted her to notify them that they'd like to support the idea financially. We're talking about full funding here; they must submit a detailed plan for everything they're going to need. Miriam said the donor wanted to remain anonymous, but she's certain it has to be one of the philanthropists they sent the email to. It doesn't even matter. Margot, your idea will be realized! Can you believe it? We are over the moon and Adrienne and I are sending you kisses! Do you see now? How important hope is? Do you see? Come on, rest these few days, so that when you come back you are ready for all the work that will be waiting for you," she said.

I couldn't believe what I was hearing.

"I think my heart just stopped beating from pure joy, Danielle," I said, barely getting the words out of my mouth.

"Likewise. See you next week, kisses," she said, ending the conversation.

I closed my eyes and couldn't contain myself. I screamed out loudly,"Well done, well done!"

You woke up asking me, "Margot, what's going on?"

"A miracle, a miracle happened Arthur."

"What miracle?"

"I don't know where to start. Do you want me to tell you?"

"Of course," you smiled at me and placed the pillow comfortably under your head, "I'm all ears," you said, and I began to tell you what happened.

We talked for an hour. It was important for me to tell you every little detail of what happened. You listened to me carefully and when I was finished you said, "I'm incredibly proud of you."

You hugged me and kissed me.

We spent almost half a day in bed, completely surrendering to our feelings. We enjoyed every moment. You kissed me all over my body and I ran my fingers through your messy, brown hair.

"I want it to be like this forever," I said.

"I know we said no plans, but tonight I want to take you somewhere and do something special," you said.

"Really? Where?" I smiled.

"It's a surprise."

"I thought I was the only one who could plan," I teased you.

"You, my dear - you live in delusion," you kissed me and got out of bed, "I'm going to get organized so we can eat something. Then we have to get ready to leave."

"Arthur, how should I dress?"

"As you wish, just take something warm to put on in case it gets chilly."

I started asking a million questions but I then stopped myself, took a deep breath, and went downstairs to get something to eat.

A few more hours passed as if they were a few minutes. The evening approached and you and I got ready for our special date.

"Do I look beautiful?" I asked as we went out.

"I'm not going to tell you something you need to know yourself," you reminded me, and I smiled.

"And how about me? Does this t-shirt match this pants?"

"Are you asking me for my opinion on clothes?" I was teasing you.

"Let's say I am," you smiled.

"It matches, don't worry."

I kissed you and we left the villa.

"Where are we going?" I asked again.

"Give me your hand," you said.

We started walking. The sky was stunning, light and dark interspersing. There were even stars out.

"Look at the sky. Heaven is so accessible to us, and we forget it," I sighed.

"The sky means freedom to me," you said, "and to you?"

"The sky means change to me," I smiled.

"Change? Why?"

"Because the sky is proof that you can change. The sky may be gray and gloomy one minute, but then it can become crystal clear. It's always changing, but we should always remember the sunny days," I said.

"Yes, when it rains, it rains for everyone, but when you cry you are the only one crying."

"A smart woman told me that absolutely everything is a personal choice, and most of all sadness and happiness."

You hugged me and kissed me hard.

"You are brave," you said with a proud expression on your face.

We kept walking and talking until we arrived at the port of Antibes. I followed you until you stopped in front of a catamaran and spoke to a man on board.

"Good evening," you said, "are we on time?"

"You're on time, Mr. Arthur. Everything's ready," he said as I looked at you, feeling exhilarated.

"Margot, this is Victor, he'll be our captain tonight," you said, pointing to the small vessel. "Victor, this is my wife Margot."

He smiled at me and nodded his head.

"Captain? Arthur? Where are we going?" I asked.

"Just relax and enjoy the ride," you said, and kissed me, "leave everything in Victor's hands."

"Arthur, I have never ..."

"I know, I know, this is your first time. Last year I tried to get you on a boat, but you refused. Trust me, you're going to love it, come on," you took my hand.

"I'm scared," I said.

"You're not scared of anything, let alone this."

Victor politely pretended not to see us or hear us, and I took a deep breath and boarded with my eyes closed.

"This is like a small living room," I smiled, as we went below deck.

"Yes, it's wonderful. Have a seat."

"Are we ready?" Victor shouted.

"Yes, let's go," you called out, giving him the go ahead. I took a deep breath as we slowly moved away from the port.

You popped open a bottle of champagne and offered me a helping of strawberries and a slice of cake.

"Cake!" I exclaimed.

"There's no party without cake, and I know that it's important for you to blow out a candle at midnight," you said, feeding me a piece.

"I never told you I like to make a wish when I blow out my birthday candles."

"You didn't have to."

"You mean you read me?"

"I read you because I want to get to know you. Is that ok with you?" your deep brown eyes shone like the stars in the sky. I smiled and you topped up my glass of champagne.

"Cheers to you!"

"For what?" I smiled.

"For inspiring me," you said, and winked.

"Cheers," I said and took a sip.

We spent a great deal of time talking to each other. I loved it so much.

"Arthur, thank you for this," I said. "Really, this is ideal."

Above deck, I looked around at the open sea, dark and exquisite, although the best part was what was happening between us.

"Tomorrow is a big day, I wanted it to be special for you."

"Tomorrow is just my birthday. Arthur, this day really was perfect. Plus, I can't believe what happened with the Barcelona Women's Network. I'm ecstatic."

"And you should be."

"Arthur, I want to tell you something. After joining the organization as a volunteer, I realized how important it is to have a fulfilling purpose. When I think about all the days I spent doing nothing - I'm ashamed of myself. It's very important for every person to have something of their own, to work on themselves, to grow as a person, to develop, and to aim for something. We're together, we're married, but that's only one part of our lives. I'm not just a wife, I'm many other things. I want to explore, to discover," the champagne seemed to push the words out of my mouth even faster.

"And the child," I said, "the child will come. And if it doesn't, we'll still manage to find joy. We're healthy, we're alive, why was it so hard for me to understand that? My focus was only on what we don't have. I forgot about everything else and you know what? The universe punishes people like that. It tells us, 'Until you learn to build happiness with what you have, I will not give you what you want, because you will destroy it too!'

My mother said it to me nicely, she said, 'Margot, do you think that once you become a mother you'll automatically become happy? No, of course not.' The dissatisfaction that swallowed me would have swallowed that joy as well, and I would have found a new reason for sorrow."

"Margot, that's behind you, behind us. You don't have to worry about that anymore. You've learned your lesson the hard way and no one can take that lesson away from you."

"Yes, it was a hard lesson, and you know what, Arthur? At the end of the day, it has never been about you. I don't have time to change you and to model you, that's not my job. It's a waste of time. My job is to take care of myself and look for the faults in myself. I felt comfortable there Arthur, in that sad room, I felt comfortable blaming you for everything that wasn't good in my life. But when I realized that everything I was expecting from you was in fact my task - I saw that I had to start changing myself immediately. The happiness I seek - it has always been in me."

"Margot, it's midnight," you said. "Happy Birthday," you hugged me tightly and kissed me. "I wish for hope to caress your soul forever," you smiled, and handed me another slice of cake, this time with a lit candle. I took a deep breath and blew out the flame.

The sky was dark and open, and the stars seemed to smile at us from above, making it even more divine. I didn't wish for anything this time, I just closed my eyes.

"I'll give you my present tomorrow morning," you said.

"Arthur, this is more than enough," I said,"I'm so grateful."

After that glorious evening we returned to the villa very early the next morning, and although I could barely keep my eyes open, I had to write this letter, not to analyze everything, but to experience bliss again.

Yours,

Margot

P.S. The champagne untangled the words in me and helped me push my thoughts out. I told you everything, and I felt like I was talking to a friend. While I was talking to you, I noticed how you looked at me and I realized – we've never been, and we'll never be enemies. The rudder of my life is really in my hands and even when you won't be able to help me get through the storm, you'll patiently wait at my side. I'll never be angry at you because I know now - every captain fights a different storm.

CHAPTER TWENTY

August 25, 2019

My dear Margot,

I know that as soon as you see this letter - everything will be clear to you. That's why I left it here, attached to the picture frame, which is in fact the secret box where you keep all the letters you never gave me. We were lucky - you didn't need to give them to me. It's true that the universe is bigger than all of us.

When you wrote the first letter and put it in the frame - a sound woke me while I was asleep in the living room. I heard something fall. I realized it was coming from the bedroom and I wanted to check if you were okay. When I entered the bedroom, I saw the bathroom door and the bathroom window were both open. I knew it was unusual for you to do that, you've told me so many times to close the door because there is a draught which comes through.

I looked at you, fast asleep in bed, and I thought that the universe must have woken me and given you the deepest sleep, because the noise didn't stir you an inch. I looked around and tried to find what it was that fell. I saw the picture frame on the ground. I knew the frame was your favorite, but you had never told me it had a secret compartment, that it was actually a hidden box. When I found it on the floor, I thought it was broken. I bent to pick it up and immediately noticed that there was something else inside. The frame wasn't broken, but it was open and there was a letter in it - your first letter. I picked it up, took the letter, and quietly left the room. I sat down on the stairs and unwrapped the piece of paper and began to read it.

You know the rest.

As the days went by I used every opportunity to read the last letter you had written. As I read them, I understood that this was how you were healing. The truth is that those letters started to heal me too. I felt that through them we started talking again, and it helped me to see my mistakes. I was ready for anything. If you'd decided to leave me, I wouldn't have stopped you, because I would've known that it was the fair result of your soul searching. I would be lying to you if I told you that I didn't fear it, but as you once told me - we cannot live life in fear. I had to let you find yourself and hope that you chose to stay. I knew that when this journey of yours ended you'd find peace, and once you found it you would not compromise your peace for anything - and you shouldn't, you really shouldn't.

I watched you grow and discover yourself. You're like this beautiful blue iris that blooms at the end of summer. Margot, I want to tell you that I'm very proud of you. Really. I'm proud that you faced yourself and that you started touching the places that hurt the most. Unfortunately, I couldn't help you with that. That was your task, it's always been your task and I'm glad you know that now. Every person should be his or her own hero because the hero we're looking for always lives inside us.

I'm also proud of you for being part of something that changes the world for the better. Your vision develops more every day. The realization of your idea to expand charitable assistance to mothers' through the Barcelona Women's Network, is proof of your incredible intuition. I'm not at all surprised that a donor decided to fund this project. It has such great potential. This donor must have a good heart.

I'm sure of this - I don't know what the future will bring, but I know that it's very important for you and I to follow our own personal path. We're not one, and we can never be one. We're two adults joined in marriage with completely different life stories, habits, desires, and fears. We must never give up our personal identity and our own dreams. I hope at some point we'll walk together in the same rhythm, following our own paths, but in the same direction.

Happy Birthday.

Yours,
    Arthur.

P.S. This is the most personal thing I've ever given to anyone. You were right - writing is not easy at all if you're looking for the truth.

EPILOGUE

August 25, 2020

My dear Mom,

I've been gathering the courage to do this for a long time. I want to tell you so many things. I know that you'll feel my words and that you'll hear me. Since the tumor was detected in your body last October, I can feel pieces of you inside me every day - more than ever.

Since the day I lost you, I've kept thinking I see you all around me. You were sick when you came to visit me in Paris before my birthday last year, and I didn't even know. You didn't tell anyone and you kept yourself in good spirits until the very end. When I found out there was still some time left, I couldn't believe it.

I asked you why you didn't tell me the doctor diagnosed you with glioblastoma when you were here, and you said it was because it was only important for you to see me and give me my birthday present. I couldn't hold back the tears. You took my hand and told me that the way our visit ended didn't bother you at all. 'If it had been any other way,' you said, 'it wouldn't have been us.' I can't get those words out of my mind, even today.

It took me a while to stop blaming myself for a lot of things because I know I wasn't a good daughter. But your departure awakened me to a completely new world, the world which you showed me. This new world freed me from all my pain, encouraging me to talk about all the wounds that hurt me, and to see that in life it's futile to think about how things might be. Every day I learned to cope by taking baby steps. I faced everything, and the pain slowly turned into something else. I'm not sure what exactly it turned into, but I know it didn't turn into resentment. I didn't allow that.

In this letter I don't want to talk about you leaving, because I can still feel you here. A friend once told me, 'When my brother passed away, his death broke me and then set me free because I realized that I was carrying him inside me, and that he's always there. Something new awoke in me, and I knew that my brother had found a place in my soul. I'm not afraid of anything now.' I couldn't understand it then, but now I understand - because I can feel you in my soul, how comfortable and warm you are.

I want to tell you about all the new things that are happening to me. My life is good. I've learned to live for myself, and that way I'm better for everyone - but living for yourself doesn't mean being selfish or thinking you're the best, it has nothing to do with that. I was most selfish when I lived the least for myself. To live for yourself means to be awake, to recognize yourself, and to constantly work on yourself.

"What will you do tomorrow?" Arthur asks me that every day, because he knows I take responsibility for my life. That feeling is wonderful.

Arthur doesn't complement me, nor do I complement him, we simply want to spend time together. There are things we enjoy doing with each other, and there are things we want to do separately. It doesn't matter at all how often we see one another, or what we do during that time. The important thing is that when we look at each other we grow and we talk. The time spent together is essential for us because we've stopped feeling like it's an obligation. We know we don't have to go somewhere every weekend or have dinner out every Friday. We do what we love. There are days when we're too busy or when one of us doesn't feel well and doesn't want to talk, and that's okay, it's human. What's important is, that when we talk, we say something sincere to each other, even if it's only a few words, that way it means a lot more. Marriage isn't our final destination, because every final destination is just an illusion in life. The world doesn't stop here. On the contrary, the world is just beginning.

The project with the organization in Barcelona was a great success. I've been there several times and when I saw how the idea developed and how many people it helped, how it changed their lives, I felt incredibly motivated.

I've already started working on other projects at Les Restos du Cœur and I find it very fulfilling. I made good friends there. We got along well from the very beginning. I'm doing what I've always wanted to do; I want to change the world for the better with my work.

And finally - Eliza! I welcomed her with such incredible ease, just as we created her - without pressure and without expectations. When she was born on the twenty-ninth of July we gave her your name and I wished for her to be a strong, brave, and independent woman like you. I wished for hope to caress her soul forever, because your soul was always so full of hope.

Eliza is the fruit of my and Arthur's life and love, she came when we knew who we were as individuals, and as a couple making a life together. She is the most precious thing that's ever happened to us. You can't deceive the universe and you can't achieve balance mechanically. I found my balance gradually when I started to choose happiness over sadness, when I started not letting pain and anger turn into dissatisfaction, and when I started to be grateful for the life I have, instead of yearning for what seemed out of reach - then and only then did my greatest wish come true.

She falls asleep with the blanket you gave me. It's hers now. Michaela says that she reminds her of you. I hope that's true. When she starts to understand I'll tell her that her grandmother made that blanket, and if she asks me where you are, I'll put her little hand on her chest and say, "Here she is. Here, where there is hope, she lives here."

I love you endlessly.

Yours,
    Margot

P.S. Now I know that in life a person can have a second birth. The first birth is when you're physically born, and the second is when you admit your own mistakes. Acknowledging mistakes is our most difficult birth, but it's also our greatest liberation. Today isn't only my birthday, today is also my second birth. Not every person can be born a second time. People who get that chance are very lucky - they taste the juice of life again, this time without all the bitterness.

As I'm writing this letter, I can't believe this is me, but looking at my smile in the reflection of the window and looking out at my garden full of blue, blooming irises - I finally recognize myself. Yes, this is really me. I am one very lucky woman.

Acknowledgements

I am thankful for having the opportunity to express myself through art. I want to thank everyone who believed in me; that has always been my biggest strength and kept me going through difficult times. I want to thank my husband for knowing me so well, even better than I know myself. I am eternally grateful to him for helping me become stronger, and for understanding that I am not dependent on anyone, not even on him.

About the Author

Ksenija Nikolova is a Macedonian fiction author. She is the author of six books, and this is her second novel translated into English. Her work is also translated into Bulgarian and Russian. She says people inspire her, and she thinks of art as an ice breaker that pushes boundaries and changes the way they see things. The world has become very judgmental and ignorant, and Ksenija believes that writing stories that smash discrimination and stereotypes can make us better and happier. Ksenija is currently working on a new novel she is very excited about. She is writing it in English and is enjoying every step of the process.

Connect with her on Social Media

Instagram : @ksenijanikolova

Twitter: @Ksenijawrites

Also by Ksenija Nikolova

All Men Love Leah

ALL MEN LOVE LEAH

A Novel

By Ksenija Nikolova

KINGSLEY

PUBLISHERS

Chapter 1

It's August and it's unbearably hot in Pisa, tourists pass by and take photographs, enjoying themselves. Everyone seems happy, maybe they are happy, or maybe they just act like they are. Nothing is clear to me. I see the sun beat down on them. I see beads of sweat form on their brows. I feel sorry for them because they must be so uncomfortable in the heat. No; I don't feel sorry for them. It's their fault. They know how hot it is, yet they go out, then they complain about the sun. I don't understand people.

I stand at my apartment window smoking a cigarette and look at the emptiness in front of me. It feels like I'm so close to the people passing by, I can almost touch them. They normally go to the Square with the crooked tower. It's the main attraction for tourists but it means nothing to me. It's just proof that in this world something has to happen all the time for something else to happen. I stand and enjoy my cigarette. I don't want to rush, even though my parents will come back from lunch anytime now. My parents don't know that I smoke. I am twenty-nine years old, and my parents still don't know that I smoke. Their opinion means everything to me. Maybe that is pathetic, but that is how it is. It works well like that to be honest. It's convenient. I get to enjoy my daily habits and they don't know I'm doing anything they don't approve of. I simply do as I please. I always do as I please.

I am obsessed with the thought that everything is absolutely in vain, and that every human being is born the way he is meant to be, and it cannot be escaped.

The tourists are very loud. They are very, very loud. I have a feeling that in their country they are not the same people. I have a feeling that they are waiting to travel somewhere to show their true selves, to laugh out loud, to shout and run in the streets. Maybe it's illogical to think that - I don't know, but I suspect it's true. Where does that joy; that serenity; that energy come from? Are these people ever sad; or are they programmed so that when they travel, they are constantly happy? I don't know. On the other hand, maybe the trip itself makes them happy, and in those moments, there is joy. I don't want to travel. It's too complicated for me. I've never been anywhere. I don't want to go anywhere; even the thought of it tires me. Don't all the cities look like each other? You can't see anything new. You just imagine that something is different, but in fact the same image, the same story is constantly repeating itself - expensive restaurants, loud tourists, long queues, and incredible congestion. It's all nonsense. I avoid it. I decide that travel is overrated.

One more drag of my cigarette and I'm finished smoking. Maybe I will have time for another smoke. Yes, I will definitely have time for another. I will light one more, and if I hear my parents coming in, I will run to the toilet. I feel good when I light a new cigarette. I wish I could smoke it in silence, but that is impossible here in the summer because there are tourists everywhere.

I look out the window and see a child with an ice cream, all dirty and running. The ice-cream is dripping but no one says anything. Is that joy? I don't understand. I look out at a woman in high heels. She can barely walk. Her feet must be sore. She must be very tired. I wonder why she does that to herself. Why she does not stay home, or put on comfortable shoes?

The woman appears at the window in front of me. She's wearing a grey coat and has long, dark brown hair. Her hair falls, hiding her face. I focus my attention on her. She runs and her coat flows behind her. It strikes me as odd. She stops to tie her coat and looks around as if she is looking for something.

She catches my gaze from where I'm standing at the window. We look into each other's eyes and she smiles, but she keeps running. After a few seconds, I lose sight of her. Her face is like a little girl's. Her stature is proud and strong, but perfect. I feel like I have seen her somewhere, I feel like I know her. I must have seen her somewhere before, but if I had, I would have remembered. I would certainly have remembered her. A woman like her is not easily forgotten, that's for sure. I consider that it's because I like her, so I feel like I know her, but

I don't really know her at all. I only know I like the way I feel when I look at her. I can't make sense of how I feel, but I look at her until I can't see her anymore.

Later, she is an image stuck in my head. I can't stop thinking about her – the mysterious woman who wears a coat when it is hot outside. I hear my parents come in. I hide my cigarette, run to the bathroom, and shut the door. I pretend to take a shower, but I'm not even thinking about what I'm doing. The woman in the grey coat is the only thing on my mind.

.   .   .

The next morning I wake up with the usual desire for the day to be identical to the previous day. It's quite common for me to feel like this. I enjoy living that way. There is nothing more beautiful than habits, consistency, avoiding any risk, ignoring the unknown. People deliberately choose the opposite and then complain that they have new problems. I'm happy I'm not like them.

The image of the woman from yesterday pops into my head again. I don't understand myself. Why is she in my head again? It doesn't make sense. It's hard to survive in my head. I know that, that's why I wonder.

I want to push time to pass by a little faster. I have always thought that time passes too slowly, and I wish someone would do something about it. I can't understand people who complain that they don't have time for anything, and that time passes too quickly. I have time for everything, and in the end I still have so much time left that I don't know what to do with myself.

My parents are going out again but I decided to stay home. My home is the most beautiful place. I watch TV, I think, I eat whatever I want, and whenever I am alone - I smoke cigarettes.

I start watching a movie, knowing in advance that the movie does not deserve my attention. There is a boring movie on TV. Every boring movie on TV is a reason for a new cigarette. I stand at the window, light one, and feel wonderful.

There are so many tourists again, running and taking pictures. They are chasing the new, hot day in Pisa; thinking they can seize it; thinking chasing the day is seizing it. I think they are fools, amazing fools, all of them! Where are they running? Why are they in a hurry?! Do they think they can change things? Do they think they can achieve anything? People are so average. People complain that they never have time because they unknowingly chase time away from themselves. Time runs away from them because they are constantly trying to hold onto it. They squeeze it with both hands, they squeeze as much fresh juice out of it as possible, and then they drink the juice, expecting a miracle to happen. It can't be done that way. It can't work that way. Everything has been decided already. Everything has been thought out a long time ago. People will never be more powerful than time. I truly pity them for being creatures full of hope.

"Hey, where are you going?" It sounds like a voice shouting at me as I close the window. It seems like the voice was addressing me. There are so many people passing by my window, I can't see who it was that spoke.

I lie down on the couch in the living room and stretch out my body. I stare at the TV. I try to make myself comfortable. Nothing happens. Nothing happens in this movie.

I try to ignore the fact that what I'm watching has no point, but I can't ignore it. My mom always tells me that absolutely all movies have a point. Maybe it's my fault. Maybe I just don't understand the movie. My mother never watches movies to understand the essence. She always focuses on the most unimportant parts. That's why it's understandable to me that for her, absolutely all films have a point. A person who doesn't seek the essence doesn't mind not finding it.

"Hey you, come to the window!" the voice from earlier calls out again. At the same time I can hear small pebbles being thrown directly against my window. I get up from the couch and go to check what it is. I don't open the window, but peer through the glass, and look downstairs.

At that moment, a small stone hits the window right in front of my eyes. For that second, I think it is going to hit me, so I open the window angrily, look below, and try to find the culprit.

I see the person responsible. It's the woman in the grey coat. She's dressed in the same coat she wore the previous day, she is smiling, and just as beautiful as I recall. She seems so full of life. She giggles and looks up at me.

"Who are you and what do you want?" I shout.

"Who am I?" she laughs, playfully.

"You have a very loud voice; loud and high-pitched. That's the worst combination. One can hear you even when you are not there," I shout. I expect her to say something, but she just keeps looking at me, and smiles.

"Tell me who you are? What are you looking for under my window?" I shout, straining my voice and getting upset.

"You are very serious, smile a little."

"If you don't tell me who you are and what you want from me, I will close the window and go inside."

"Okay, okay, don't get angry, calm down," she laughs, and it makes me feel self-conscious.

"Do you even know why you're laughing?" I ask, straining hard. I want her to hear me, but I strained so hard I think I might lose my voice.

"I laugh because life is beautiful; and you, why don't you laugh?" she continues in her high-pitched voice. Her voice is impossible to ignore, just like the boring movie I was watching a while ago.

"I don't laugh, because I'm smart enough to know that life can't be beautiful if it isn't easy."

"How sad," she says.

"I'm closing the window. Whoever you are, I'm glad I didn't meet you," I say, trying to close the window.

"Alright," she shouts in that shrill voice, and it seems to me that all the people passing by her stop for a moment.

"Please don't scream at me like that anymore!" I say.

"I am Leah," she says.

"I am Enzo; and so now what? What do you want from me, Leah?"

"A cigarette; I saw you smoking. I saw you yesterday too."

She says it like I am a small child who did something bad, and who must ask her for forgiveness.

"I saw you yesterday too. It was impossible not to. You walked past me wearing that grey coat, and I still don't understand why you're wearing it. It's hot outside, its summer you know?"

"I know, but I like coats."

"Why?"

"I like it because it's plain. It doesn't reveal anything

187

about my personality or my character, so nobody can make assumptions about me just from looking at me. You know how people are- always judging you from what they see on the outside. I don't want to be judged by superficial things. Almost nobody wants to look deeper than what they see with their eyes. I don't like that, so I like to wear plain things. I hide the core of me, my essence, for those who want to search for it."

I look at her looking at me, not able to understand what is happening to me. I can't escape the way I'm starting to feel about her. She's absolutely perfect in my eyes. Every one of her dark hairs falls into place, every part of her body seems to move to the rhythm of some beautiful music, and from her gaze it seems a river full of emotion flows. Her energy is so strong and seductive. I look at her impatiently, looking forward to meeting her, and I want to tell her that.

"Leah, there are two things I could not ignore today. The first is the boring film on television and its non-existent point. You are the second thing, the greatest essence, whose core I can see even now, but I fear I will not be able to understand you."

Chapter 2

Leah got under my skin. We meet, and from that day I spend every day with her. She is so deeply ingrained in my consciousness that I don't think I will ever be able to drive her out of my thoughts. I'm fine, and at the same time I'm scared. Everything feels new to me; she takes me to places I didn't even know existed and gives me a completely different view of the world. She complicates my life in one way, yet simply makes me happy in another.

We walk the streets of Pisa; we run; we play; we laugh. We don't touch; we don't kiss; we're not intimate at all, and yet we have something incredibly intimate. We live life. We do everything those people I watched from my window do; those people who I thought were crazy. I don't feel too hot in the sun. I even forget that it's summer. I walk around breathless without realising it. I exist in the moment. I feel like I can change things I don't like, and I find such things beautiful now. Every second I'm happy, every second is different from the previous moment, and for the first time in my life, time passes so fast that I want to pack time into a suitcase to hold it still.

"Are you okay?" Leah asks me.

"I'm fine," I smile with a shy look.

"That is the most important thing, that is what people live for, only for that," she tells me.

The truth is I know absolutely nothing about Leah, except that she is beautiful, young, and irresistibly alive. Time passes too fast and I desperately want to stop it from running away from us. As time ticks, questions form in my mind. I want to know everything about her, yet I feel that I already know everything I need to know.

"How someone makes you feel is the most intimate thing you can know about that person. Everything else is less important," she will say almost every day.

"I agree," I will say, looking at her, "but I am in love with you and I want to know everything about you, even the things that are less important. Is that a sin?" I will mutter when she does not listen to me.

My parents don't know about us, but they can see the changes in me. I think that makes them happy. I'm rarely at home these days. I start to have my own life, and I'm not afraid to live it. At home, my mother regularly gives me little smiles as she sits in the living room or the kitchen, and my father pats me on the shoulder when I go out. I know that means they're happy because they know I'm happy too.

Pisa is still crowded with summer tourists, and the number just keeps growing. I can't believe that Leah and I are pushing through the crowd every day, and I don't even mind it. Leah enjoys it. She's like a feather. She passes through the crowds easily, gently, slipping through. I see the way she moves and I love her even more. I want her. I need her, and it excites me in a strange way.

"Do you want to go to the beach?" she asks me out of the blue. I look at her and feel embarrassed. I can't swim and I don't how to tell her. I act like I'm not interested.

"Where?" I ask. It will be so crowded and surely the water is dirty."

"Anywhere, come let's go to Marina di Pisa. It's so beautiful there," Leah insists.

"I don't know Leah, I don't feel well," I say, although Marina di Pisa is one of the places everyone wants to go to. Who doesn't want to leave the city to go to the beach?

"Come on, why aren't you feeling well? Is there a reason?" she asks, probing.

I have a million reasons why I don't want to go of course, but I don't want to tell her any of them. I'm too shy.

"You know what, you may have your reasons, but you certainly have at least one reason good enough to come with me," she laughs.

I tell myself I have to stop focusing on all the reasons that make me feel scared. Normally when I hesitate to do something, I focus on the reasons why I don't want to do the thing, and those reasons always win. Maybe though, those reasons don't actually win, but I allow them to win.

I smile at Leah and stop arguing. I decide to try something new instead. I decide to go along with her, even though I know that I won't know how to act when we get to the beach, but there is an important reason why I want to go. The reason is that I have never done anything before that was not dictated by my fear. I have always fed my fear, caring for it more than for myself, giving it strength to grow inside me more and more, eventually swallowing me. I decide this time, I will act differently.

Marina di Pisa is only ten kilometres from Pisa. It is a nice small place, with beaches, restaurants, and bars. Tourists love to go there for walks in the harbour. In the summer season the place is full. Everyone goes there to relax and enjoy themselves. Leah gave me instructions on what to bring along, but I felt incredibly nervous.

"Look how wonderful it is, and you didn't want to come! Lucky you have me," Leah says as she laughs, dragging her large, colourful beach bag.

"Where did you get this bag? It's a strange looking bag, and that hat!" I tease her.

"I have a complete set of hats," she says, "didn't you notice?"

"No."

"You see everything, but in fact you don't see anything."

"I only see the surface of things remember. I'm superficial," I reply, teasing her.

"You're not superficial, you're far from superficial. You're scared of the depth in things, so you float to the surface," she looks at me, and I am speechless. "Here, we can stay here, this is enough space for us, and it's close to the water."

I don't reply. We lie down on my big, green towel. I'm hoping she doesn't bring up going into the water, because it's a conversation I want to avoid.

"Let's go swimming, come on!" she shouts impatiently as she takes off her linen dress, revealing a sexy bathing suit beneath it. The bathing suit barely covers what it needs to.

"Don't you think your swimsuit is too provocative?" I look at her. She is glowing like the sun, ready for play.

"Don't be boring, let's go for a swim!" She runs to the sea like an excited little girl, fearless, not fighting the water but loving it. She folds into the waves naturally, and the sea accepts her as if she were a part of it. It is effortless perfection to watch. She goes in deep, until I can no longer see her.

I try to enjoy the beach and forget about the fact that I don't know how to swim. I stretch out on my green towel and close my eyes. The sun caresses me and I surrender to the warmth. I am sinking into another world. I forget everything. I forget where I am. I feel like a bird in a tropical region. I am colourful and I am painted with the most beautiful, bright shades. It's impossible not to notice me and not to admire me, but I'm different from the other birds. It's a pity, but I don't know how to fly.

I feel droplets of water trickle me in places on my body. I wake up from my wonderful dream, and I see Leah standing beside me, squeezing water from her beautiful, long, dark hair, dripping over me.

"What are you doing?" I ask her.

"Why don't you come in and swim?" she laughs.

"I can't swim," I blurt out.

"There is no such thing," she says.

"There is such a thing. Look, I can't swim."

"I know you can swim, I know. Come on!"

"Leah, stop."

"Come on Enzo, come on."

"Leah, I can't swim, okay. I don't know how to. I don't know how to swim." She looks at me with her blue eyes, as deep as all the seas. She looks at me with a dull stare.

"Why didn't you tell me Enzo? Why hide it from me?"

"I didn't think it was important."

"It's important. Swimming is important."

"I don't understand you. You're confusing me."

"Swimming is a symbol of fearlessness. Swimming means swimming through problems and through obstacles. It doesn't matter how you swim, but it's important to try. It's important to have a goal and not to give up. It's not about the damn swimming in the sea. It's about swimming through life, through struggle, into truth, into your truth, into what you believe in!"

That's what I love most about Leah. She knows what to say, and she knows how to say what I don't like to hear. She knows how to touch me, and she does it without hurting me.

"I have never even tried," I am embarrassed to say.

"There is no time like the present. Let's try now. I will stand beside you. I promise I will be by your side the whole time, and nothing will happen to you," she extends her hand to me, looking at me with her beautiful eyes, full of sincerity.

We walk to the sea and I put my feet in the water. I can't believe what I'm doing - but I keep going. Leah holds my hand and slowly pulls me forward.

"You won't drown, it's impossible; and do you know why- because, instinctively you'll want to be saved, believe me. You won't let anything bad happen to you," she says.

I listen to her and keep going deeper and deeper. The water hugs me halfway, and I'm afraid, but I don't show it. I keep going in deeper, and I don't turn back. I go forward. Leah is smiling. I focus on her warm face. She gives me strength that I couldn't imagine. The water reaches my neck and Leah starts swimming, still holding onto me with one hand. She does not let me go.

"I will be right here all the time, don't worry, but try to let go Enzo. Try it alone, try. Whatever happens, I'm here. Come on, learn to swim. Learn to depend only on yourself, come on, you can, I know you can."

I can still reach the bottom of the water with my feet. I keep going forward and I know that in a short time, I will not be able to stand. I'm scared, I'm terribly scared, but I try not to think about it. I think of the worst, but then I think of the best. I decide to hope. I close my eyes, and I feel the sun caressing me. I hear Leah's gentle voice.

My feet can't feel the bottom of the water anymore. The water gets too deep to stand, and I let go of Leah's hand. I start moving my arms the way I think I should, and I kick with my legs, trying not to sink. It's hard for me and I swallow some water, my head sinks a little, but I don't give up. I take a breath and move on. I try keeping my head above water in one place, without swimming forward. I kick my feet and somehow I stay on the surface. My arms hurt, my legs hurt even more, but I keep going. I manage to find some balance. I have been alone in the deep sea for a few minutes and I haven't drowned yet. It gives me the strength to move on. I see Leah swimming. She doesn't say anything but I know she's proud of me. I know her silence means she's pleased. I smile. I feel incredible strength and desire. I feel like I'm full of courage. I want to start moving forward, to start swimming, so I kick and use my hands as shovels, scooping and scooping through the water. I breathe. I see the light and I breathe. I inhale oxygen as I scoop water and move. I don't stop. I don't turn back. I focus on my goal. Leah looks at me and waves her hand.

"Congratulations," she shouts. "You learned to swim!"

I smile, and I'm still doing fine. I keep moving, using my hands as paddles. I keep scooping water like I'm digging a hole in the sea. I'm not fast, but I try. I'm not perfect, but I'm swimming.